"I don't think it's a good idea for you to work here," he said.

"I don't work for you," Lily said. "I work for your mother. When she's ready for me to leave, I will. In the meantime, she needs the help, and I like working for her." And if she could find another job that paid as well, she would leave in a heartbeat. Being around Trace was harder than she'd ever imagined. "And I'd appreciate it if you didn't do that again." She wiped the back of her hand over her still tingling lips.

"Do what?" he asked, his blue eyes smoldering as he stared down at her.

"You know damn well what."

"You mean kiss the ranch hand?" The corners of his mouth quirked upward.

I started this book around the time my mother was diagnosed with pancreatic cancer. I finished it in a fog after she passed away. Losing a parent is never easy. I still find myself reaching for the phone to call her and talk about something, anything and sometimes nothing much at all. I just want to hear her voice one more time. This book is for her. If not for her love, support and encouragement, I might never have become an author. She was my first proofreader and cheerleader. She loved reading and always had a book in her hand. When I was a teenager, she worked at the library in our small town and came home with sacks of books to read. I got my love of stories and my artistic flair from her. I also got my love of the color orange from my dear mother.

Though I miss her, she will live on in my heart.

Dear Mom, I'm wishing you bright colors and sunshine, and all the paint your brush can hold.

HOMICIDE AT WHISKEY GULCH

New York Times Bestselling Author

ELLE JAMES

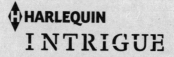

HARLEQUIN
INTRIGUE

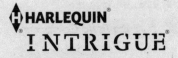

ISBN-13: 978-1-335-40147-2

Homicide at Whiskey Gulch

Recycling programs
for this product may
not exist in your area.

Harlequin Enterprises ULC
22 Adelaide St. West, 40th Floor
Toronto, Ontario M5H 4E3, Canada
www.Harlequin.com

Printed in U.S.A.

Elle James, a *New York Times* bestselling author, started writing when her sister challenged her to write a romance novel. She has managed a full-time job and raised three wonderful children, and she and her husband even tried ranching exotic birds (ostriches, emus and rheas). Ask her, and she'll tell you what it's like to go toe-to-toe with an angry 350-pound bird! Elle loves to hear from fans at ellejames@earthlink.net or ellejames.com.

Books by Elle James

Harlequin Intrigue

The Outriders Series

Homicide at Whiskey Gulch

Declan's Defenders

Marine Force Recon
Show of Force
Full Force
Driving Force
Tactical Force
Disruptive Force

Mission: Six

One Intrepid SEAL
Two Dauntless Hearts
Three Courageous Words
Four Relentless Days
Five Ways to Surrender
Six Minutes to Midnight

Ballistic Cowboys

Hot Combat
Hot Target
Hot Zone
Hot Velocity

SEAL of My Own

Navy SEAL Survival
Navy SEAL Captive
Navy SEAL to Die For
Navy SEAL Six Pack

Visit the Author Profile page at Harlequin.com.

CAST OF CHARACTERS

Trace Travis—Delta Force soldier on leave to support his mother after the murder of his father, the rich owner of Whiskey Gulch Ranch.

Lily Davidson—Girl from the wrong side of the tracks, tainted by her parents' choices in life and in love with the only man she can't have. Working as a ranch hand on the Whiskey Gulch Ranch.

Joseph "Irish" Monahan—Former Delta Force soldier who left active duty to make a life out of the line of fire.

Matt Hennessey—Motorcycle-riding auto mechanic and former marine and town bad boy.

Roy Gibson—Foreman of the Whiskey Gulch Ranch.

Rosalynn Travis—Trace's mother and newly widowed ranch owner, desperate to find her husband's killer while trying to run a ranch without much help.

Oswald Young—New owner of the Rocking J Ranch, determined to create a hunters' paradise.

Chad Meyer—Neighbor and owner of the Rafter M Ranch.

Chapter One

Master Sergeant Wade "Trace" Travis moved into position a block from the designated alley where they were to collect the dead drop. Darkness had long since descended on the Afghan city of Jalalabad.

They'd arrived inside the city near dusk, driving a nondescript van. They'd worn the traditional loose clothing of the Afghan male over their operational uniforms. On their heads, they'd chosen to wear the triangular *karakul* hats.

Trace had driven the small team into the city. Staff Sergeant Levette "Levi" Warren had ridden shotgun. Staff Sergeant Joseph "Irish" Monahan had been dressed similarly but relegated to the back seat.

Dressed as locals, they hadn't drawn attention and had found a quiet alley to park the van not far from their dead-drop location. They'd waited until nightfall to shed their outer garments, don their helmets and communications devices, and take up their arms. Levi was the only man on their team who remained dressed in the traditional Afghan garb.

Trace turned to Irish. "You ready to perform your last mission with Delta Force?"

Irish snorted. "Couldn't let me sit this one out, could they?"

"Are you kidding? Special Operations Joint Task Force wouldn't let you out of the theater without one last hurrah." Trace grinned.

"I couldn't believe your name came up when they tagged us with this dead drop," Levi said. "It's pushing your luck. You're bugging out. Why tempt fate?"

Irish shrugged. "It's just an intelligence gathering mission, not an assault operation. We'll be in and out. No big deal."

Trace prayed that would be the case. If he had some wood to knock on, he would have. Because Irish was forty-eight hours away from a flight back to the States. His luck could be bad and jeopardize this short mission.

Trace rubbed the lucky Susan B. Anthony coin he kept in his pocket. It was the one his dad had given him to ward off danger. He'd never considered himself superstitious until he'd joined Delta Force ten years ago and witnessed luck in action. Training was key to performance, but luck, fate and faith had played a part in seeing him through many missions. He'd watched more than one man on the cusp of redeployment back to the States get assigned to a mission and not make it out alive to return home to his family.

"Tell me again why you're getting out of the army?" Levi asked.

Irish laughed. "I've been deployed more times in my career than I care to count. Each mission seems to get more and more dangerous. Hell, we never know for certain who is friend and who is foe."

Levi nodded. "True. But you knew that before volunteering for Delta Force."

"I know." Irish adjusted the strap beneath his chin. "I'm just ready to live life out of the line of fire. Look at us." He pointed to Trace and Levi. "What do we have to show for all we've done in Delta Force? A couple of medals for missions we can't talk about. When was the last time you kissed a girl?"

"I kissed one last time I was at Fort Bragg," Levi said.

Irish crossed his arms over his chest. "Yeah? What was her name?"

Levi shrugged. "I don't remember."

"Exactly," Irish said. "We don't have wives for a reason. We're never home to nurture a relationship."

"Some of us don't want wives," Trace said. The only woman he'd ever loved had sent him into the military having cheated on him. He hadn't found another woman he cared about or trusted enough to make her part of his life.

"Yeah." Irish's lips firmed. "But some of us want a wife, children and the house with a picket fence."

"What are you going to do for a job when you get out?" Levi asked.

Trace already knew. He and Irish were from the same part of the country.

Texas.

"I'm going to work with animals," Irish said.

Levi's bark of laughter filled the van, grating on Trace's nerves. "How's that going to help you get a woman?"

"I have to figure out life after the military before I bring a female into the mix. I've had enough of fighting people. Animals aren't as difficult to figure out. Besides, I need the time to unwind and decompress. I'm no good to any woman the way I am now." He hefted the submachine gun in his hands. "All I've known for the past ten years is killing. What skills do I bring to civilian life? None."

"What kind of animals are you planning on working with? Dogs, cats, guinea pigs?" Levi snickered. "Going to work in a pet store?"

Irish shook his head. "Horses and livestock. I'm going to find a ranch to work on. Good, honest work."

"How does that kind of work pay?" Levi asked.

"Not worth a darn," Trace said. "Not as a ranch hand."

"I'm not going into ranching to make money," Irish said. "I want the quiet time and to lower the stress level."

Levi snorted. "You'll be bored after a week."

"I could use a little boredom. Beats being shot at." Irish nodded toward Trace. "How long are you planning on staying with this gig?"

Trace shrugged. "I haven't thought about it."

"You grew up on a ranch. Don't you ever want to go back?" Irish asked.

"Someday." Trace looked away. He'd wanted to go home the day he left. He missed the life, he missed his mother. And since he'd left, he'd come to grips with his feelings for his father. The man had wanted the best for his only son. That hadn't included being involved with Lily Davidson, daughter of one of the worst families in the county. Hell, though she'd cheated on him, he missed Lily.

"Don't you miss working with livestock?" Irish gave Trace a chin lift. "I know you used to ride horses. Don't you want to ride like the wind and not worry about taking a bullet because you're out in the open?"

Too many times to remember, Trace had dreamed of riding Knight Rider, the black stallion he'd raised from a colt and trained as a cutting horse. As far as he knew, the stallion was still alive and well. His mother kept him abreast of what was happening on the ranch through her long, handwritten letters, delivered once a month, like clockwork. "I miss it," he admitted. "But not enough to quit the army." Quitting the army would mean he'd have to go back to Texas. Back home. His father might construe his quitting as a sign of weakness or failure.

Trace had joined the army to prove to his father he didn't need the family fortune, and that he could make his own decisions and be successful in his own right.

Granted, he would never be as rich as his father, not working for the army. But he was rich in friendship, honor and integrity. He was part of something even bigger than Whiskey Gulch Ranch. He was in the business of protecting an entire country. How much bigger could his contribution get?

Too bad his father hadn't thought much of his decision to join the army. It didn't matter. That had been eleven years ago. He'd barely spoken to his father since, other than the few times he'd been home on holiday.

Over the years, James Travis had mellowed and actually expressed his version of pride in his son's achievements. But he'd expected Trace to return home once he'd "gotten the need to prove himself" out of his system.

As an only child, Trace was expected to take up the reins when his father chose to retire from actively

running the large cattle operation and his other invest-
ments.

Trace knew how to run the ranch and the other busi-
nesses in which the Travis family were involved. Hell,
he'd been groomed from birth to handle the family fortune. That wasn't the issue. His father would never turn
over the reins. He'd be involved with the daily operations until the day he died.

Pulling his head out of the past, Trace focused on
the task ahead. "It's getting dark. Time to get this party
started. In and out. No drama."

"That's right," Irish agreed. "All we need to do is retrieve the dead drop and get back to the base."

Levi grabbed his sniper rifle and tucked it beneath
the long folds of his disguise. "I'll be in touch." He
slipped from the passenger seat and out into the alley.
Moments later, he'd disappeared to find his way to the
top of a building overlooking the dead-drop location.

Trace gave Levi ten minutes to get into place. When
he didn't report in, Trace spoke softly into his radio mi-
crophone, "Levi, report."

"In position on top of the building opposite the dead
drop," Levi said through Trace's headset. "All clear."

"Moving in." Trace motioned for Irish to leapfrog to
the corner of the alley they'd been directed to by Military Intelligence.

They were supposed to gather the information from
a metal box left in the alley. Military Intelligence had
indicated the message had been left by a Taliban in-
sider who was intent on revealing the depth of traitor-
ous activities.

They'd performed this type of mission on numerous
occasions. Only half had gone without a hitch. Trace

prayed this one was in the boring, no-hitch category. Irish deserved a nonevent for his send-off.

Once Irish was at the corner of the alley, Trace moved up to his position and started past Irish into the dark passageway between the buildings.

"Oh, no, you don't." Irish's hand shot out, grabbing Trace's arm. "Let me go first."

"I'm going in," Trace said and tried to shake off Irish's hand.

"That's not how it works, and you know it." Irish pushed past him. His weapon at the ready, he eased into the darkness.

"The box is ten feet in front of you," Levi said from his position above them.

Trace had Irish's back, as did Levi. But they couldn't account for what the man might find in the box. For a long minute, Trace held his breath, a heavy sensation settling in the pit of his belly.

Something wasn't right about the mission. No one had attempted to stop them. In fact, the streets had been deserted. No guards had fallen asleep at their posts, no children cried in the night. Nothing.

"It doesn't feel right," Trace murmured into his mic.

Irish paused. "I'm almost there."

"Hold up," Trace said.

"I've got nothing up here," Levi reported.

"That's just it," Trace said. "It's too easy. It's too quiet."

"Yeah. I've got a chill running the length of my spine," Levi admitted. "What do you want to do?"

"Abort," Trace said. "Pull back, Irish."

"Man, I'm within reaching distance of the box," Irish said. "What if that message is important?"

"It's not worth losing your life over," Trace said. "Abort."

For another long moment, Irish hesitated. Then he sighed. "You're the lead on this mission." He turned and took several steps toward Trace. He hadn't gone more than a couple yards when a loud explosion shook the ground beneath Trace's feet.

Trace was thrown backward, landing hard on his back, the wind knocked from his chest. He fought to drag air into his lungs. Though he could tell someone was talking to him, he couldn't make out the words over the loud ringing in his ears. He sat up and shook his head. His weapon lay on the ground beside him.

What the hell had happened?

Then he noticed Irish lying facedown, sprawled in the alley.

Trace's heart raced as he pushed to his feet, grabbed his weapon and lurched toward his friend. He staggered a few steps, tripped over his own feet and fell hard on his knees, his head spinning.

"Irish!" he called out, his voice sounding as if it were coming from down a very long tunnel. He got to his feet again and forced his legs to carry him to where his teammate lay on the ground.

"Trace? Irish?" Levi's voice sounded in Trace's ear.

"I'm okay," Trace responded. "Irish is down." He felt for a pulse and breathed a brief sigh. "He's alive."

"Then get him up and out of there," Levi said, his tone urgent. "We've got company."

Trace shook Irish gently. "Hey, buddy, nap's over. Gotta get you outta here. There's a chopper with your name on it taking you to Bagram Airfield to catch your flight home."

"You don't have time to talk him into leaving on his own two feet. Get up and out of there. Two trucks full of heavily armed militants less than a block away," Levi reported. "Damn. They're climbing out of the trucks, headed our way."

Trace shook back the dizziness. He propped his and Irish's weapons against a wall, grabbed one of Irish's arms and rolled him up over his shoulder in a fireman's carry. With Irish's full weight bearing down on him, he reached for their weapons, turned and half walked, half ran to the end of the alley.

Levi met them at the corner, slung the two weapons over his shoulder and held his out in front of himself. "Go. I've got your back."

Trace had no way of protecting himself or Irish. All he could do was get his friend out of there as quickly as possible. Levi had to do the job of fending off a dozen militants.

Praying Levi would be all right, Trace headed for the extraction point outside the village.

By the time he reached the edge of the stone, mud and stick buildings, he was breathing hard and his shoulders ached with the weight of his teammate's inert body. But he couldn't stop. Not yet. He had to get to the helicopter.

Five Delta Force operators ran toward him. One split off and came to help Trace.

"Don't worry about us," Trace grunted. "I'll get Irish to the chopper. Help Levi. He's knee-deep in bad guys."

The five men ran past him. Moments later, gunfire lit up the night.

Trace remained focused on getting his friend to the

chopper. The others would follow, once they had the situation contained.

His legs shaking, his lungs burning, Trace staggered up to the helicopter. The copilot jumped down to help the medic take Irish from Trace and lay him out on the floor of the Black Hawk.

"Give me a weapon," Trace shouted.

The medic tossed him his M4A1 rifle and went back to work on Irish.

Trace turned and ran back toward the little town and the continued sharp report of gunfire. Before he reached the village walls, three members of his team who had passed him minutes before came running from the village.

"Where's Levi?" Trace shouted.

"Beck and Jimmy are covering for him." Sergeant Parker Shaw slowed to a stop beside Trace. "We've called in an airstrike. They told us to get out."

"Not without Levi, Beck and Jimmy."

"They were the ones who told us to get out," Parker said. "Levi nearly took a shot at me."

"Not leaving without them," Trace said and ran toward the village.

Parker fell in step beside him.

More gunfire sounded as they neared the village.

Then the night erupted in a fiery explosion, knocking Trace backward. He staggered but regained his footing and resumed his forward movement.

Parker rolled to his feet and kept pace beside Trace.

"I see movement ahead," Trace said.

What looked like a clump of moving parts emerged from the village into the open.

Trace could make out two men holding up a third

between them, running while twisting around to fire rounds to their rear. Several bogeys popped up over the tops of the walls.

"They need help." Within two hundred yards of the compound, Trace dropped to his knee, aimed his rifle and fired at one of the men perched at the top of a wall. The man slumped and fell from the wall to the ground.

Another explosion rocked the landscape as a round from an unmanned aerial vehicle, driven by a young air force lieutenant back at a base in Nevada, slammed into the village.

The three Delta Force soldiers running toward him staggered but remained upright, pushing forward to their destination.

Parker dropped down beside Trace.

Soon, the other two Delta Force members set up a line of fire to either side of Trace and Parker.

Jimmy, Beck and Levi made it past them and onto the helicopter waiting to extract them.

Another round smacked into the wall of the village. The enemy element who'd been firing at them lay dead or had scattered.

"I'll cover," Trace said. "The rest of you get to the chopper."

"Not going without you," Parker said. "The rest of you…move!"

"We'll go together, or not at all," Jimmy's voice rang in Trace's ears.

Overruled by his team, Trace rose and ran backward toward the waiting Black Hawk. The last man to climb aboard, he hovered close to the door, his weapon aimed at the village and any possible bad guys who might decide to take a shot at the chopper as it lifted off the ground.

The helicopter rose into the air, but not nearly fast enough for Trace. Not until they were well away from the village did Trace let go of the breath he'd been holding and turn toward his friends.

The medic worked over Irish. He had Parker applying pressure to a wound while he established an IV of fluids.

As soon as he had Irish stabilized, he turned toward Levi.

"Don't worry about me," Levi said. "Just a flesh wound."

Beck was wrapping Levi's leg in gauze. "Yeah. Right. The man bleeds like a stuck pig."

"I'll live," Levi said. "Thanks to you guys." He winced as Beck tied a knot over the wound.

The medic had the pilot call ahead to have the medical staff ready to receive the wounded.

They were met by a military ambulance, and Levi and Irish were loaded into the back.

"I want to go with them," Trace said to the driver.

"Not enough room," the driver said, closing the back of the van.

Trace looked around for transportation to get him to the hospital. A captain dressed in a clean uniform hurried toward him. "Are you Master Sergeant Wade Travis?"

With a frown, Trace nodded. "I am."

"I'm Captain Williamson. Your CO heard you would be here and wanted me to personally contact you."

"Should I know you?"

"No, sir. I'm a chaplain."

Trace stiffened. "Our guys are going to be okay. The medics are taking care of them."

"I'm not here about your teammates," Captain Williamson said.

He might not have been there about Levi and Irish, but the rest of Trace's team gathered around him. When a chaplain singled you out, it was never good news.

Parker, Beck, Jimmy and the others stood beside him.

"Could we talk in private?" the chaplain asked.

Trace's heart squeezed hard in his chest. He squared his shoulders and lifted his chin. "You can say anything in front of my team."

The chaplain stared from Trace to the men surrounding him. "Are you sure?"

With a nod, Trace braced himself. "What's on your mind, Captain Williamson?"

Glancing down at a paper in his hand, the chaplain took a deep breath and faced Trace. "Your father was murdered two days ago. You've been recalled home."

Chapter Two

"There's a truck coming up the drive." Lily entered through the back door of the ranch house into the kitchen.

Rosalynn Travis worked over the stove, tossing ingredients for a beef stew into a stockpot. "Cross your fingers this applicant knows which is the business end of a cow." She turned off the stove, wiped her hands on a dish towel and hurried toward the front of the house.

Lily grabbed the shotgun from the corner of the kitchen and followed her boss.

The older woman was out the door before Lily could catch up.

A man with scraggly, oily hair and dirty jeans dropped down out of a beat-up pickup and walked toward the porch.

Lily pushed through the screen door and called out, "That's far enough."

The man ambled to a stop.

Rosalynn crossed her arms over her chest. "What's your purpose?"

"I'm Randy Sweeney, and I'm here about the job I saw advertised at the feed store," the man said and smiled through crooked, blackened teeth. "This is the

Whiskey Gulch Ranch, isn't it? And you *are* advertising for a ranch hand, aren't you?"

Rosalynn nodded.

He hooked his thumbs through his belt loops and rocked back on his heels. "I'm here to apply for the job."

Rosalynn shot a quick glance toward Lily, before returning her attention to their applicant.

"When was the last time you worked on a ranch?"

"Well, now, ma'am, I ain't actually worked on a ranch, but how hard can it be? You poke cows, ride horses and get fed by pretty girls." His gaze slid to Lily, who'd moved up to stand beside Rosalynn.

Rosalynn shook her head. "Sorry, mister. The advertisement specifically asked for experienced ranch hands. We don't have time or the inclination to train anyone."

Instead of turning to leave, Randy took a step forward. "I understand you ladies need a man around the ranch. I'm pretty handy in a fight."

"We're not planning on having a fight," Lily said.

"Ain't you Brandy Jean and Marcus Davidson's little girl?" The man's smile turned into a sinister smirk.

"I am." Lily's jaw firmed, and her hands tightened on the shotgun. "Not that it's any of your business."

"Heard you'd come to work for the Travises." The stranger scratched his chin. "Didn't expect you'd still be working here after old man Travis's death." His gaze slid from Lily back to Rosalynn. "Thought for sure his old lady would have sent you packing by now."

Lily raised the shotgun in her arms, her eyes narrowing.

Rosalynn snorted. "I'm not old, and Lily isn't leaving. She's been more help to me than any of the worthless ranch hands who've deserted us since my husband's death."

"You'd better leave now before I put a load of buckshot into you." Lily raised the shotgun up to her shoulder and aimed it at the man on the ground in front of her.

Randy shook his head. "You ain't gonna pull the trigger on a gun that'll knock you back on your pretty little bottom."

Lily aimed the shotgun a little to the man's left and pulled the trigger. The blast jerked her shoulder back, but she remained standing. "As you can see, I can pull the trigger and still remain upright. What's more important... I *will* pull the trigger." She aimed the gun at Randy. "Leave...now."

His brows dipped low. "Just because you have a gun doesn't make you all that."

"No?" She raised an eyebrow. "And just because you're a man and I'm a woman, you think you're smarter and stronger than I am?"

Randy snorted. "You're not like your mama, are you?"

"Not in the least," Lily responded.

"Damn shame." Randy hitched up his jeans. "Two women... Alone on a ranch... You're asking for trouble."

"We aren't asking for anything but a ranch hand who knows ranching. Whether male or female. And you're not the one." Lily jerked her head to the side. "I'll give you three seconds to get in your truck."

Randy took another step forward. "Or what?"

Lily fired off another round, pulled shells out of her pocket and reloaded in seconds. "The next one will be aimed at your body." She raised the shotgun to her shoulder and pointed it at his midsection, then lowered it slightly. "Want to test me? Think I won't do it?"

Randy stood his ground for a moment, his eyes narrowing even more. "You'll regret this."

"I regret that I've wasted two shells," Lily said. "I won't waste another."

"I'll leave, but you're setting yourselves up as targets. Two women running a ranch as big as Whiskey Gulch won't cut it. You'll fail."

"At least we'll fail at what we know how to do, without supporting someone who knows nothing about ranching," Rosalynn said. "Go home, Mr. Sweeney. We're looking for experienced help."

He snorted and turned toward his truck.

Another truck headed toward them, kicking up a tail of dirt on the road leading up to the ranch house.

"Great," Lily muttered. "Another loser come to apply for the job."

Randy hesitated with his hand on the door handle of his pickup.

"My finger's getting itchy," Lily said.

"I'm going." Randy yanked open the door and stepped behind it without getting in. His gaze followed the truck headed toward him.

Lily would rather have had Randy off the property before she had to deal with another *applicant*, but the man wasn't making a move to leave and now had the truck door between him and her buckshot.

A shiny black pickup pulled to a stop beside the beat-up one. The sun glinted on the windshield, keeping Lily from seeing the face of the driver.

"Whoever it is will get one warning." Lily held the rifle against her shoulder and aimed at the newcomer.

The driver stepped out of the truck and rounded the door, his dark hair and blue eyes instantly recognizable.

All of the air left Lily's lungs and her heart stopped beating for a full three seconds. Then it slammed against her ribs and raced, pushing blood and adrenaline through her veins.

The last person she'd expected and the one she least wanted to see strode toward the ranch house. "That's a helluva homecoming for a man who's been away for more than a year."

"Lily," Rosalynn said. "Put down the gun. My boy is home." The older woman ran down the stairs and enveloped her only son in a hug so tight, it had to be cutting off the air to his lungs.

Meanwhile, Lily had forgotten how to breathe and that she was aiming a shotgun at the man and his mother.

"What's *she* doing here?" Trace asked, his chin lifting toward Lily.

His mother glanced back, tears trickling down her face. "Lily works for me."

"Since when?"

The sound of his voice brought back a flood of memories and emotions as Lily lowered the shotgun. "Since the last time you were here, over a year ago," Lily said, finding her voice, infusing judgment into her words. Since then, things had changed.

"She started as my housekeeper," his mother said, "and now she's my one and only ranch hand."

"What happened to the rest of them?" he asked, his

gaze shifting from his mother to Lily, his eyes narrowing.

"The men spooked when your father was murdered." Lily snorted, her lip curling back. "They left, thinking the murderer would be after them next."

"Bastards," Trace said. He tilted his head toward the man standing by the old truck. "Who's he?"

"Nobody." Lily glared at the man in question. "He was just leaving."

Randy pushed away from the door of his pickup. "Did I hear right? Are you James Travis's son?"

Trace nodded. "I am."

The man stepped forward, his arm outstretched. "Randy Sweeney. I'm here answering an ad for help. Maybe you're the one I need to talk to."

Trace ignored the man's hand. "The ranch belongs to my mother. What she says goes."

Randy dropped his hand to his side.

"She said to go," Lily said between clenched teeth, her hand tightening on the shotgun.

Randy raised a finger. "Not really." Then he pointed the finger at Lily. "*You* told me to leave."

"Is that what's holding you back?" Rosalynn Travis gave Randy a tight smile. "Then let me make myself clear… You are trespassing on private property. Leave now, or I'll call the sheriff."

The man looked from Rosalynn to Trace as if he didn't quite trust her word.

"You heard my mother," Trace said. "Leave—and don't come back. The Travis family doesn't suffer fools."

Randy bristled. "You calling me a fool?"

"If the shoe fits…" Trace left the statement open.

When Randy refused to move, Trace took a step forward, his fists clenched.

Randy backed away. "Some say Mr. Travis was killed by someone he knew." He shot a glance at Rosalynn. "Most violent crimes are committed by people close to the victims. Usually family members."

"Not in this case," Lily said through clenched teeth. "We'll find whoever murdered Mr. Travis." She lowered her voice and stared at Randy with narrowed eyes. "And make him pay."

Randy raised his hands. "Don't look at me. I didn't do it. I was just looking for a job. Those can be hard to come by in these parts."

"Not for folks who know how to work hard," Rosalynn said.

"You sayin' I don't know how to work hard?" Randy asked, his lip curling on one corner.

"She's saying get off her property," Trace said. "Now, get in your truck, or I'll help you get there." He took a step toward the other man.

"I'm going." Randy hopped into the driver's seat of his old pickup, slammed his door and revved the engine. A moment later, he'd reversed, spun around and headed down the gravel road, spitting up a cloud of dust in his wake.

Lily relaxed her hold on the shotgun but retained the tension in her body as she faced the man she'd loved from the day they'd met in grade school. The one man she couldn't have. The man she'd lied to in order to get him to leave.

By the look on that beloved familiar face, he hadn't forgotten what she'd done to him all those years ago.

She squared her shoulders. Trace needed to hate her.

What they had ignored as children and teens couldn't be ignored as adults. They didn't come from the same backgrounds. No amount of wishing could change that. She would never fit into his world. Not with her parents' criminal backgrounds.

Not that he'd ever want her back in his life.

Lily sighed and turned toward the ranch house. "I'll pack my bags."

"The heck you will." Rosalynn moved to stand in front of her, blocking her way into the house where she'd taken up residence since she'd come to work for the Travis family. "I can't afford to lose you, Lily. Please, stay." The older woman turned her attention to Trace. "And you." She poked a finger at her son. "This young woman has been a godsend to us over the past year. I don't know what I would have done without her."

Trace held up his hands. "I'm not telling her to leave. She's a grown woman, she can make up her own mind. Although, I don't know why she's living here when she has a husband to go home to."

Lily stiffened.

Before she could say anything, Rosalynn jumped in. "Husband? What husband?" Rosalynn turned a crooked smile toward Lily. "Does he know something I don't?"

Lily shook her head. She'd always been straightforward with Trace's mother, never wanting to hurt the mother of the man she loved. But she hadn't told her the lies she'd used to drive Trace away from Whiskey Gulch Ranch. "I don't know what he's talking about. I'm not married. Never have been." She met his gaze dead-on, daring him to repeat the lies she'd told him all those years ago.

TRACE'S ANGER BUBBLED up in his chest and threatened to spew from his mouth. He clamped his lips together and ground his teeth. He refused to blast Lily in front of his mother, who apparently thought the younger woman was an angel incarnate.

He'd wait until he could get Lily alone to get answers from her. Not married? Part of him rejoiced at the news. The other part boiled with anger. She'd told him she was in love with Matt Hennessey, and Trace was too straitlaced for her. That had been eleven years ago. They'd been teenagers. Why couldn't he let it go?

Lily lifted her chin, gave Trace one last glance and turned toward his mother. "We need to get moving if you want to get to the funeral home before they close."

Rosalynn nodded. "You're right." She reached out and patted Trace's cheek. "I'm sorry you had to come home to this. Your father was so proud of what you'd accomplished in the military. He didn't say it to you, but he bragged about you to anyone who'd listen." Tears welled in his mother's eyes. "I'm glad you made it home for his funeral."

The knot in his gut hardened. "I'm sorry I wasn't here. If I had been, maybe this wouldn't have happened."

His mother's eyes widened. "Or you could have been the target along with your father." She shook her head. "You can't second-guess the past. It's done. All we can do now is move on." She closed her eyes, drew in a deep breath and let it out. When her eyes opened, she was the mother he remembered, who shouldered burdens during hard times and marched forward. "I have to meet with the funeral director. You can come with me, or not. It's up to you. I won't judge."

His chest tightened. They couldn't bring his father back, but he could be there for his mother. "I'm coming."

"I'll drive," Lily said.

"The hel—" Trace started.

"Trace," his mother said with that stern expression she'd used on him when he'd been a recalcitrant child. "Lily's been driving me since your father's death. I feel comfortable with her behind the wheel. Let her."

His fists clenched, but he didn't argue. His mother had been through enough. "Very well."

"Besides, it will give us a chance to talk."

"What vehicle are you taking?"

"Your mother's SUV," Lily said.

His mother hurried to explain. "I couldn't bring myself to get into the truck. It was so much a part of who he was."

Trace shook his head. "All I knew coming home was that Dad was murdered. I got here as soon as I could. I haven't heard all the details."

Lily followed Rosalynn into the house, calling out over her shoulder, "I'll fill you in on the way. We really need to get moving."

Rosalynn patted Lily's arm. "Thank you, dear. I admit to being a little disoriented lately."

"That's to be understood." Lily pulled Rosalynn in for a quick hug. "You've been dealt a huge blow. Losing someone you love is never easy." She herded Trace's mother through the house, pausing in the kitchen to cover the pot of beef stew. It could wait, uncooked.

Rosalynn walked to a hook on the wall where a man's suit hung, complete with a white shirt and a navy blue tie. She lifted the suit and held it against her chest.

She chuckled, the sound catching on a sob. "He hated wearing suits. But he was a stickler for tradition and would have insisted on being buried in one."

Trace's gut clenched. Seeing his mother's grief brought it home like nothing else. His parents had been married for almost forty years. More than half their lives. He held out his hand. "Want me to take the suit?"

She shook her head. "No. I've got it."

On their way through the house, Lily grabbed Rosalynn's purse, looping it over her shoulder. She snagged her own and headed back out the door, brushing past Trace as she went.

The scent of honeysuckle wafted beneath his nose. Seriously? She still used the same honeysuckle-scented shampoo as she had all those years ago?

With the scent came a myriad of emotions and images crowding into his memories.

Images of Lily lying with her head across his lap, staring up at the endless stars in the Texas sky all those years ago, her voice soft as she named the constellations and the planets. When a meteor streaked past, she'd close her eyes and make a wish.

Trace would bend over and kiss her lips and she'd chuckle.

"I got my wish," she'd say.

"What did you wish for?" he'd ask.

Every time, she'd respond, "For a kiss from the guy I love."

That was just one of the memories pushing to the forefront of his recollections. There were so many more he'd shoved to the back of his mind to keep from going off the deep end. He'd loved Lily Davidson more than life itself. When she'd dumped him for the town bad boy, Matt Hennessey, she'd shattered his heart into a million pieces. Her announcement had been the final straw that had pushed him into leaving home and joining the army.

His father had started him down that path by trying to dictate his life as soon as he'd graduated high school. He was supposed to stay on Whiskey Gulch Ranch and assume more responsibilities of ownership without any actual authority. His father could never release the reins enough to let his son make decisions.

After they'd butted heads too many times to remember, Trace and his father had had a massive argument. His father didn't think him worthy of running the ranch. He hadn't liked Trace's choice of a girlfriend. James Travis was a man who followed rules and laws. Lily came from a family of lawbreakers. She'd drag Trace down and hold him back in whatever he decided to do with his life. If he didn't drop her and start towing the line on the ranch, he would have to move out and find another way to make a living.

That was when Trace had finally realized he needed the freedom to grow into the man his father never believed he could become. He'd never be that if his father ran the show. Having had enough, he knew he would never earn his father's respect until he'd been successful on his own. That day he'd visited an army recruiter, signed the documents and sworn into the army.

With a week to go before he shipped out, he'd gone to Lily and asked her to wait for him. He'd explained that his next step was to go to the Military Entrance Processing Station, where he'd start the paperwork for a security clearance and go through mental and physical evaluations before he shipped out to basic combat training.

The people performing the background checks for the security clearance might come to his hometown and ask questions of the people who knew him to gauge whether or not he could be entrusted with protecting the nation.

That was when Lily had hit him with the news that had ripped his heart out. She'd been seeing Matt Hennessey and had fallen in love with him. She wasn't planning on waiting for Trace to return. She wanted to get married immediately and it was to Matt she'd given her heart.

Trace had felt like she'd punched him in the gut so hard, he couldn't catch his breath. The woman he loved didn't love him like he'd thought she did. When he left Whiskey Gulch, he'd have nothing to bring him back but the occasional visit with his mother.

He'd gone into the army with a desire to prove to dear old Dad that he didn't need his money to survive. Trace Travis could make it on his own. As far as making it on his own, he didn't need a woman in his life to cause him more pain. Lily had crushed the life out of his heart. For the next eleven years, he would hold up her example to any woman he met and judge them based on what they had never done, but what they might do in the future.

Trace couldn't take another beating like he'd taken that day. He didn't need the constant reminder with Lily living and working at Whiskey Gulch.

He helped his mother into the front passenger seat and then climbed into the back seat of his mother's SUV on the opposite side from Lily. His position gave him a good vantage point from which to study Lily without her knowing.

She hadn't changed much since they were teenagers. The soft curves of her cheeks had become more defined. Her face had slimmed, and she wore her hair in a French braid instead of the ponytail he used to love pulling. She'd inherited her beauty from her mother. Thankfully, she hadn't followed in her mother's footsteps.

Brandy Jean Davidson had married Marcus Davidson when she was sixteen and got pregnant with Lily. Her parents had kicked her out of the house, convinced their oldest daughter would be a bad influence on their three younger children. Brandy Jean and Marcus's marriage lasted only until Lily was born. Marcus wasn't ready to settle down and take on the responsibility of raising a child. He joined a motorcycle gang and left the town of Whiskey Gulch, Texas, for California.

Without a high school diploma and no work experience, Brandy Jean went to work at a strip club. She barely made enough money to support herself and Lily, living in a run-down trailer on the edge of town. She found she could make more money off the dance floor. Lily might not have had the best home life, but her mother had tried to insulate her from her business. She wasn't always successful.

Lily pulled out of the yard and headed onto the gravel road leading to the highway. Once they were on the paved road, Trace's mother filled Trace in on what had happened. "Your father was shot while out riding fences." Her voice broke.

Lily reached across the console and squeezed his mother's hand. "Want me to finish?"

His mother nodded and swiped at a tear slipping down her cheek. "Please."

"Your father was hit several times. He fell from his saddle." Lily took a deep breath. "His foot caught in the stirrup and he was dragged all the way back to the barn. The sheriff said at least three rounds hit him. It wasn't an accidental shooting. Someone was aiming at your father."

"When he made it home, he was conscious for only a few seconds before he passed. His foot was still caught." His mother's voice hitched. She stared out the front window. "I couldn't get him down. It wasn't until Roy returned from town that I got his foot out of the stirrup. By then the ambulance had arrived." She swiped away a tear. "Too late for James."

Roy Gibson was the foreman who'd come to work for his father after Trace had joined the army.

His mother shook her head and turned in her seat so that she could see Trace. "Your father didn't have a chance. Someone murdered him."

Rage burned inside him. Though he'd had his differences with his father, he'd never stopped loving him. Unclenching his fist, he reached over the back of the seat and touched his mother's shoulder. "I'll find the bastard who killed him," Trace vowed.

"*We'll* find him," Lily corrected.

Too angry to argue, Trace let her comment pass.

His mother laid her hand over his. "It won't bring him back."

"No, but the killer can't get away with what he's done," Lily said.

"He has to be caught," Trace said. "He's killed once. If he's not held accountable for what he's done, what's to keep him from killing again?"

Chapter Three

What was to keep the killer from killing again? The thought roiled around in Lily's mind along with the fact Trace was sitting behind her in the same vehicle. She'd never expected to be this close to the man again. After she'd dumped him so brutally all those years ago, she didn't think he'd want to be in the same breathing space with her.

His father's death had taken precedence over any revenge or avoidance dance concerning her. For all she knew, he might not be giving her a second thought. Eleven years was a long time to forgive and forget.

Lily hadn't forgotten one thing about Trace. He was still the man she'd fallen in love with. She hadn't met another who could take his place. From what she could get out of his mother without asking point-blank, Trace hadn't married, nor had he brought a significant other home to meet the parents.

"What happened to all the ranch hands who worked for Dad?" Trace asked. "And where's Roy, your foreman?"

"Since your father was murdered," Lily said, "rumors have gone around the community that Whiskey

Gulch Ranch has been targeted, and anyone having anything to do with the ranch could be murdered as well."

"Roy had an accident a few days ago," Trace's mother said. "His brakes failed. He blew through a stop sign in town and smashed into a tree to avoid hitting a family in a minivan. He suffered a damaged foot. He wanted to come back to work right away, but I told him to wait at least a week to keep it up and give himself time to start healing."

Lily picked up from there. "After Roy's accident happened, the ranch hands quit outright or called in sick, indefinitely. Some said their families had been threatened."

"Who's been taking care of the animals?" Trace asked.

"You're looking at us," his mother said. "If not for Lily, I don't know how I would have managed."

"So far, we've only been able to care for the horses, cattle and smaller livestock near the house and barn," Lily said. "We don't know what's going on farther out. If someone is threatening the ranch hands, what else are they doing that we haven't seen?"

"As soon as we're back from the funeral home, I'll ride the fences," Trace said.

"You can't go alone," his mother said. "You need someone to watch your back."

"I don't need help," Trace insisted. "I work better when I don't have to worry about others."

His mother shook her head. "You're taking one of us or you're not going at all."

Lily glanced at Trace in the mirror, a smile tugging her lips.

His mother had used the tone she'd used when she'd

been talking to the younger version of Trace so many years ago. She'd always made him go with his father or with a friend, insisting on a buddy system to keep from being stranded out in the middle of the ranch with no way of getting back or sending anyone for help.

"Mom, I can take care of myself," Trace said. "Besides, if one of you goes with me, the other is left exposed to whoever is trying to sabotage the ranch."

"Going out on the ranch alone got your father killed," his mother said. "I don't know what I'd do if you were targeted next. You can't go out alone."

"I'm going to pick up Roy from the hospital tomorrow," Lily said. "He can stay with your mother at the house while you and I check the fences and start the search for your father's killer. Your mother will be safer at home."

"I don't need anyone to ride shotgun with me," he said.

"If you don't take Lily, I'll send her out after you anyway," his mother said. "Now, quit arguing. You're making my head hurt."

"And we're here," Lily pointed out as they rolled through town and came to a stop in front of the funeral home. She parked in the lot at the side of the building and climbed down.

Trace got out and opened his mother's door.

Rosalynn sat for a long moment staring straight ahead, clutching the suit, without moving.

Trace touched her arm. "I can meet with the funeral director. You can stay in the car."

She shook her head and turned. "No. I have to face this sooner or later." With a deep breath, she accepted Trace's arm and let him help her out of the vehicle.

Lily's heart hitched in her chest. James Travis had made it clear from the moment Trace brought Lily home to meet his parents that he didn't approve of Trace dating her. Though Trace hadn't mentioned it, she knew from the grapevine that he'd had a major argument with his father over her. Shortly afterward, he'd announced he was thinking about joining the army to get the hell out of Whiskey Gulch and away from his father.

Lily had never wanted to come between Trace and his father. That their argument had escalated to the point Trace felt it necessary to leave Whiskey Gulch Ranch meant his father had given him an ultimatum.

She understood the senior Travis's reservations about Trace dating her. Everyone in the county knew who she was, and more important, who her mother was. On more than one occasion, Trace had stepped between Lily and someone who thought that because she was Brandy Jean's daughter that her body was for sale as well.

Trace had a couple of scars to show for his interference. Lily had been grateful he'd been there to help, but she'd gotten good at defending herself. As soon as she could navigate the internet, she'd studied Krav Maga. When she was old enough to drive, she'd taken lessons in the art of self-defense from a retired Delta Force soldier. Trace had found out and insisted on taking her to and from her lessons. Lily hadn't been surprised to learn Trace had gone into Delta Force. He'd been impressed by retired Sergeant Major Ketchum, or Ketch, as his students were allowed to address him.

Mrs. Travis led the way into the funeral home, holding her son's arm.

The funeral director met them in the lobby. "Mrs.

Travis, thank you for coming today. And thank you for bringing Mr. Travis's clothing." He took the suit and held out a hand, taking hers into his grasp for a long moment. Then he released her hand and turned to Trace. "Trace, it's good to see you back in town."

"Thank you, Mr. Miller," Trace said and shook the man's hand.

"I'm so sorry for your loss and grateful that you were able to get here so quickly to be with your mother in your time of loss." The funeral director released his hand and stood taller. "Thank you for your service to our country. Your father must have been so proud of you."

Trace's jaw tightened. "Thank you for seeing to our family's needs. What more do you need from us?"

He led the way into a conference room and waited for them to be seated before settling into a chair at the end of the table. "I need to know your preferences on the casket and music. Your burial plot has been located and is being prepared. Do you have any photos you'd like to use in the video?"

The more questions the director asked, the more Rosalynn slid down in her seat.

When Lily could stand it no more, she spoke up. "If you have a list of what you expect from us, we can go through it at home. Mrs. Travis has selected the casket. I believe that was the main reason she had to be here today. So, if you'll excuse us, we have to get back to the ranch." She jotted an email address onto a slip of paper and handed it to the director. "Send us your list or your questions, and I'll compose an email with the answers."

The funeral director smiled briefly. "Of course. The

funeral is in two days. I'll need your answers no later than noon tomorrow in order to complete preparations."

"You'll have it," Trace said.

"Viewing is tomorrow evening," the director said. "You'll want to get here early so that the family has time to visit before others arrive."

"We'll be here," Rosalynn said.

Trace helped his mother to her feet and guided her out of the room and to the exit.

Once outside, Rosalynn drew in a deep breath and let it out. "I don't know what came over me. I just suddenly couldn't breathe."

"We're headed home. You can rest when we get there. Trace and I will take care of the chores," Lily assured her.

"I need to help," she said, her hand on the door handle to the SUV.

Trace brushed her hand aside and opened the door. "I'm here now. You need to let Lily and me take charge of the ranch."

"Trace is right," Lily said. "Besides, I'm sure there will be people who want to know about the funeral arrangements. Someone will need to be in the house to field those calls."

Rosalynn sighed. "You're probably right."

"You've done enough over the past three days," Lily said. "Let us take care of things. You need to rest."

"I'm not an invalid," Trace's mother said.

"No, but you've lost someone dear to you. It's emotionally and physically draining," Lily pointed out. "I don't know how you've held up, other than out of sheer cussedness." She smiled at Rosalynn. On the outside, Rosalynn had been a rock since the sheriff had delivered the news of her husband's death. She had to be coming apart on the inside.

A motorcycle pulled up beside them. The man driving it wore black jeans, a black T-shirt and a leather jacket. He dismounted and pulled off his helmet.

Lily braced herself. Of all the people to show up, why did Matt Hennessey have to come at that exact moment?

Matt strode up to Rosalynn. "Mrs. Travis, I just got back into town and heard about your husband." When he reached for her hands, Trace stepped between them.

"Hennessey," Trace said, his face stone-cold, his jaw tight.

"Travis." Matt's eyes narrowed. "I was speaking to your mother."

The tension in the air was thick enough to cut with a knife.

Lily touched Matt's arm. Matt had been her friend when no one else in the small town of Whiskey Gulch would have anything to do with her. With a background similar to hers, he'd been on the fringe of the social spectrum as well.

The bastard son of a woman who worked as a bartender at the local watering hole, he'd grown up with a rough crowd of hoodlum teens. He'd ridden a motorcycle, worn his hair a little long and sported a five o'clock shadow all day long. Sexy and dangerous, he was every girl's secret fantasy. But not Lily's. She'd been in love with Trace since she was in sixth grade.

Matt shook her hand off his arm and met Trace's glare with one of his own.

Rosalynn gripped her son's arm. "Trace, please."

For a moment, Trace stood his ground. Then he stepped back, never losing eye contact with the other man.

Rosalynn smiled at Matt and took his hands. "Thank you, Matthew."

"Let me know if there's anything I can do to help. If you need anything fixed, I can fix anything with an engine and I'm not bad with a hammer."

"That's sweet of you," Rosalynn said. "I might need your help if anything breaks down. With James gone—" she swallowed hard "—and Roy's broken foot, we're shorthanded, and although I'm good with the animals, I'm hopeless with mechanics."

"I'm home now. I'll take care of things," Trace said.

Rosalynn nodded but smiled at Matt. "Thank you, Matt. You're so kind to offer."

"Say the word and I'll be there to help," Matt said. His gaze shifted from Rosalynn to Trace, his jaw tightening. "I can be out at the ranch in less than ten minutes." He turned to Lily. "How are you holding up?"

She nodded. Matt was her friend, and she appreciated his concern, but having him in the same breathing space as Trace could be disastrous. "I'm sure you have other things to do."

Rosalynn smiled and turned toward Trace. "Matt has his own repair shop now. He's quite good at fixing things. He can take something other people have given up on and make it come alive again."

Trace gave the hint of a nod, but his expression was tight. "I'm sure he can."

Matt frowned. "I get the feeling you don't like me. What did I ever do to you?"

Lily's heart leaped into her throat. Now was not the time for her lies to surface. She stepped around the two men and hooked Rosalynn's arm. "We'd love to share in this little reunion between you two men, but we need to get Mrs. Travis home before it gets dark. It's been a difficult day."

"Thank you, dear." Rosalynn patted Lily's hand. "I am tired and there are animals to be fed and laundry to be done. Thank you for stopping by, Matt. The funeral is the day after tomorrow." She climbed into the back seat of the SUV.

Lily didn't have the time or energy to deal with the two men. "When you're done puffing out your chests and posturing for dominance, we can get going."

Finally, Trace shifted his glare from Matt to Lily.

"Oh, good," she said, her voice tight. "I've got your attention. Can we go now?"

Trace gave Matt a narrow-eyed stare and said in a low tone, "Stay away from my family."

Matt snorted. "Your mother can speak for herself and Lily isn't yours. You gave her up when you ran off to play soldier."

Trace's hands clenched into fists and he stepped toward Matt.

Lily gave Matt a slight shake of her head.

"I'm not the one who ran out on her," Trace said. "You are."

Matt frowned. "Don't know what you're talking about."

Her heart hammering, Lily did the only thing she could. She threw up her hands and made a scene. "Fine. You two can stand around and be all stubborn, hard-headed and male. I'm taking Rosalynn home. She doesn't need whatever bull you two are throwing at each other. Trace, if you don't want to walk back to the ranch…" She shrugged and marched around the SUV to the driver's side, praying he wouldn't continue the argument or throw a punch at Matt. She climbed in, started the engine and pressed hard on the accelerator without putting it into gear. The engine revved loudly.

For another long moment, the two men stared at each other.

Then Trace turned and climbed into the SUV.

Lily shifted into gear and drove away from the funeral home.

"What was all of that about?" Rosalynn asked. "Am I missing something I should know? Did you and Matt have a falling-out I don't know about?"

"No, Mom," Trace said, his voice tight as if he were talking through gritted teeth.

Lily bit her tongue. Now wasn't the time to fill her boss in on the lie she'd told her son. She wasn't sure she'd ever let her know. Rosalynn had enough trouble on her plate with her husband's death and the threats they'd had to the ranch. And she didn't need to be reminded that Lily had once loved her son.

Hell, seeing Trace again…stubborn and cranky as he was…

She shot a glance at the man in the seat beside her.

He stared straight ahead, his arm resting on the window ledge, his fists clenched. Trace liked to be in control of the driving. He always had.

Lily's lips twitched.

He had to be gnashing his teeth with her behind the wheel.

She drove out of Whiskey Gulch, the town that had been named after the Whiskey Gulch Ranch.

For the first few minutes, silence reigned.

Deep in her thoughts and memories of better times with Trace, Lily was jolted back to the present when Trace asked, "What else needs to be done on the ranch besides checking the fences?"

"Plenty of things, I'm sure," Rosalynn said. "James had mentioned the hay would be ready soon. It will need to be mowed, raked, baled and stored before it rains."

"Trace and I can manage the mowing, raking and baling, but we'll need help storing the rectangular bales in the barn. Otherwise, it will take days to accomplish."

"I'll see what I can do to muster up some ranch hands," Trace said.

"Good luck." Lily snorted. "I've never seen such a bunch of scaredy-cats in my life."

They were turning into the ranch before Lily knew it. The sun had dipped to hover above the horizon, heralding the end of the day in a startling display of color.

Lily shielded her eyes as she drove the length of the gravel drive to the ranch house. Her pulse quickened as she was reminded that she'd be sleeping under the same roof as Trace. In the room next to his.

Sweet heaven, her heart pounded against her ribs. Why was she so worked up? It wasn't as if they were a couple anymore. That was ancient history. He hadn't shown any sign of attraction or desire for her. He was over her.

The problem was, she wasn't over him.

As soon as Lily parked the SUV beside the house, Trace was out and helping his mother from the vehicle.

"I really can do this on my own," she said.

"I know, Mom, but humor me." Trace smiled down at his mother and walked with her into the house.

As soon as she'd set her purse down, she headed for the kitchen. "I'll rustle up something for dinner while you two take care of the animals."

"Are you going to be all right?" Trace asked.

She gave him a watery smile. "What choice do I have? We have a ranch to run. I don't have time to fall apart."

"And it's not like you to lose it." Trace leaned down and kissed his mother's forehead. "We'll be back in less than an hour."

"Take your time. I started a beef stew, but I'd like to make some corn bread to go with it." She waved him toward the door. "Go on. Lily's likely out there mucking stalls already. That woman is a dynamo. I didn't know what a gem she was until I hired her to take care of the household chores."

Trace paused with his hand on the back doorknob. "Why did you hire her, Mom?"

She shrugged. "I needed help cleaning, since I was doing all the cooking for the hands."

Trace frowned. "What happened to Cookie?"

His mother smiled. "He was getting old, so he retired. He and his wife moved to Florida to be closer to their daughter."

His heart squeezed hard in his chest. Cookie had been with them since Trace could remember. Cookie's daughter, Teresa, had gone to school with Trace. She'd married straight out of high school and moved from Texas to Florida with her husband. He remembered how sad Cookie had been when she'd left.

"I'm glad he was able to retire and move close to his daughter," Trace said. "If you need us, yell. We won't be far."

"I'll be okay. Hurry before Lily does all the heavy lifting. She's a hard worker and stubborn." His mother smiled. "I don't know what happened between you two, but you let a good one get away."

"We were kids. And that was a long time ago."

"Just saying," his mother said.

Trace exited the house and hurried toward the barn. There was no reason he couldn't work with Lily. What they'd had was long ago and better left forgotten. Since there were no ranch hands, he'd have to make do with Lily.

As he entered the barn, his pulse quickened.

The brushing sound of a rake scooping through muck led him to a stall where Lily was up to her gum boots in soiled straw.

She didn't hear him at first. When she looked up, her eyes widened briefly.

"Where did you start?" Trace asked.

"I worked the first two stalls yesterday." She pointed to the other side of the barn. "The six stalls on the other side need cleaning and the rest of the stalls on this side haven't been mucked for a week, from what I can tell. I turned the horses loose in the paddock behind the barn until we can finish the job. The other rake is hanging on the wall by the door. The second wheelbarrow is out back of the barn." Lily dug into the straw and flipped a pile of dirty straw into her wheelbarrow, her eyes on her work.

For a moment longer, Trace watched Lily, admiring the strength in her arms and her determination to get the job done. She'd always been willing to work, no matter how hard the task. It was one of the reasons he'd fallen so hard for her. Most women he'd known since wouldn't do what Lily was doing for fear of getting dirt beneath their fingernails or, Lord forbid, breaking one.

Trace grabbed the wheelbarrow from outside and went to work cleaning the six stalls on the opposite side of the barn. Every once in a while, he'd catch a glimpse of Lily. Once, he'd found her staring back at him.

Since she hadn't married Matt Hennessey, did she still have good memories about the time they'd spent together as teens? Did it matter? Did he care?

Unfortunately, he found himself caring too much. Over the years they'd been apart, he hadn't been able to move on. Perhaps working side by side, he'd finally be able to let go of the woman who'd haunted his thoughts. He hoped it wouldn't take long for him to get over her. At that moment, his desire was nearly as strong as it had been eleven years ago. He didn't have time to work through his feelings. He had a ranch to run and his father's murderer to locate and neutralize. If he wanted help, he needed men who had skills similar to his. If they had ranching experience, that was a bonus.

As soon as he got back to the ranch, he got to work, making phone calls to the men he knew or had known in the past. He was banking on the strength of brotherhood. He needed his team now.

Chapter Four

Over the next couple of days, Lily kept busy between James Travis's viewing and funeral, taking care of the house, and helping out with the animals. To the best of her abilities, she avoided Trace as much as possible. With her bedroom next to his, she couldn't elude him completely. Knowing he was on the other side of the wall left her sleepless and on edge. Only a few feet separated them physically. But the emotional chasm between them might as well have been as wide as the Grand Canyon.

He barely talked to her, although he worked alongside her in the barn and as they took care of the animals. Gone were the times they would run laughing into the stalls, stopping to kiss and hold each other. They'd been young, in love, happy to be alive and with each other.

James Travis had never liked her. He'd met her in the barn one day when she'd been waiting for Trace to join her for horseback riding. He'd told her she wasn't good enough for his son and that he would never make anything of himself as long as she was around.

He'd known his son was considering joining the military. He'd blamed her for Trace's interest in leaving Whiskey Gulch. If she insisted on staying with him, her background would keep him from getting his security clearance. She'd ruin his career in the army before it started.

When Trace walked in on his father telling her these things, Trace had blown up. He'd told his father to stay out of his life and he'd stay out of his.

That day Trace had loaded Lily into his truck, taken her home, and then driven to the nearest US Army recruiting station and enlisted. The staff sergeant who'd taken Trace's information informed him that he'd have to complete clearance forms and a background check.

Still shaking from that encounter with James Travis, Lily let the patriarch's words sink in. If she stayed with Trace, she would hold him back. She'd never been in trouble with the law, but her mother had been arrested on multiple occasions for prostitution. Her biological father was in prison for armed robbery. She'd been so afraid her parents' legacy would taint her and thus him in his background check. Once again, the sins of her parents were impacting her.

Lily had known for a long time that Trace had a need to get out on his own. He'd been talking about joining the military since he started high school. As soon as he graduated, he wanted to leave Whiskey Gulch Ranch and make it on his own. His father kept such tight reins on the ranch that, if he stayed, Trace would never be allowed to make decisions for himself.

From Trace's first mention of joining the military, James Travis had discouraged his son's decision. He'd assumed Trace would stay and eventually run the ranch, his inheritance.

Trace knew better. He would never run the Whiskey Gulch Ranch until his father died.

As Lily listened to James Travis that day, she'd come to the realization that Trace needed to get away from his father. If he didn't, he would grow to hate the man even more, and possibly hate himself.

The only way he'd make it past the background check was if she wasn't in the picture with her family's checkered past. He'd said he'd get in, go through bootcamp and advanced training, then he'd send for her. As close as they'd become, if she'd tried to break up with him, he'd still try to convince her to wait for him.

She stopped seeing Trace and quit calling him over the next few days. It was the only thing she could think to do. Lily paid a visit to Matt, hanging out with him, watching baseball with him and taking a selfie photo with him. They'd been friends for a long time. He hadn't seemed to think anything of it.

When it came time to let go, Lily had hated lying to Trace. But it appeared to be the only way to get him to leave and ensure his background check passed without the hitch of her and her parents. So, she'd waited until he was scheduled to ship out for in-processing and then broken it to him that she wasn't going to wait for him. She wanted to remain in Whiskey Gulch and she'd been having an affair with the sexiest hoodlum in town, Matt Hennessey. She was going to stay and marry him.

At first, he hadn't believed her and blamed the fight with his dad for her sudden change of heart. Then she'd showed him the photo of her and Matt in his trailer, sitting on his leather sofa drinking beer.

To say Trace was angry would have been an understatement. He'd been so mad, his face turned a ruddy red. He'd gathered his duffel bag, turned and climbed aboard the bus that would take him to San Antonio's

Military Entrance Processing Station and his future in the army.

Lily had cried all the way back to the run-down shack where she'd lived with her mother.

She didn't see Trace for five years following that fateful day. Then for the next six years she'd only caught glimpses of him from afar when he came back to Whiskey Gulch to visit his mother.

As far as she'd known, he'd never patched his relationship with his father, and he hadn't spoken to her.

That morning, she was out in the barn, cleaning the hooves on one of the registered quarter horse mares James Travis had been so proud of.

Lady was temperamental and impatient with the process, but she'd collected a number of rocks and sticks and needed them cleaned out before she developed sores and went lame.

After the fourth time Lady jerked her hoof out of Lily's hand, she straightened her aching back and shook her head. "I get it. I'm not as good at this as James or Roy, but it has to be done."

"Leave her to me," a voice said from the door to the barn.

Lily stiffened. Though he stood blocking the sunlight, and his face was shadowed, he was unmistakably Trace.

Her heart skipped several beats and then raced ahead. "I can do this. It just takes time."

"Leave it," he said, his tone more direct, unbending and final.

A spark of anger rose up her chest. She marched across the barn. "Look, you can't do everything, but since you think you can, go for it." She held out the handle of the horse hoof pick.

When he took it from her, his fingers brushed against hers, making her pulse beat faster and her knees tremble.

She backed away too fast and stumbled, teetered and flung out her arms as she fell.

Trace reached out, grabbed her hand and yanked her forward, slamming her against his chest. He held her there until she regained her balance, and then a little longer.

Her pulse pounded as she glanced up into his familiar yet unfamiliar face. Trace had been the boy with whom she'd fallen in love in grade school. He was still the same person, only he wasn't a boy anymore. His shoulders had broadened, the soft curves of youth had hardened in the planes of his face and his arms were steel bands wrapped around her waist.

Lily found it hard to catch her breath, realizing it had nothing to do with how tightly he held her but how pinched her heart was inside.

How different would her life have been if she'd asked him to stay in Whiskey Gulch and move in with her. They could have found an apartment or a little cottage to rent. He could have gone to work on one of the other ranches, or as a carpenter's assistant. She'd worked as a waitress. Between the two of them, they could have survived.

Looking at him now, she knew she'd done the right thing. He'd needed to get clear away from his father, the ranch and the small town of Whiskey Gulch. As the son of the richest man in the county, he never would have shaken the stigma of being the spoiled rich kid.

She looked at him, really looked at him. He was harder, more confident and a man his father would have been proud of. It was too bad James Travis never got to tell him. He'd expressed his pride to Lily, if not directly to his son, and regretted the distance between them that kept him from telling Trace how he felt to his face.

Trace's hands tightened around her waist, warm, strong and steady. They sent ripples of awareness throughout her body, making everything inside her burn.

"You said you were going to marry Hennessey," Trace said. "Why didn't you?"

Like ice water splashed in her face, he brought her back to reality. She pushed against his chest. "It doesn't matter."

His grip tightened, trapping her. "Did you ditch him because he wasn't good enough?"

She held her chin up and stared into his gaze. "It's really none of your business."

Trace lifted his hands, sliding them up her back to tangle in the hair at the base of her skull. "Did he make you moan when he held you?"

Her breathing came in ragged gasps. Pressed against him, she couldn't ignore the way her body reacted. She was on fire, her core burning with desire. She had no words. None could move past her frozen vocal cords.

"Did he kiss you until you melted in his arms?" he whispered, his mouth descending to hover over hers.

"No," she murmured, the sound swallowed by the crush of his lips against hers.

At first she remained stiff in his arms.

But as his mouth moved against hers, she melted against him. If he hadn't been holding her, she would have slipped bonelessly to the floor, her knees unable to hold her weight.

His tongue traced the seam of her lips.

She opened to him as naturally as if she were a flower opening its petals to the sun. Greedily, she drank him in, her tongue sweeping against his, caressing, thrusting and tasting this man she'd loved so much she'd pushed him away to explore a better life without her.

After what seemed like an eternity and yet a blink of an eye, he raised his head, abandoning her mouth.

Lily drew in a shaky breath and sagged against him. This couldn't be happening. It shouldn't be happening. Trace didn't love her anymore.

"Bet he didn't kiss you like that," he said, his voice gravelly and sexy as hell.

His words brought her back to earth with a jolt. She pressed her hands against his chest and pushed.

When he still didn't let go, she drew in a deep breath and let it out. "Let go of me."

As if he just realized he was still holding her, he let go suddenly and stepped away from her.

"I don't think it's a good idea for you to work here," he said.

"I don't work for you," she said. "I work for your mother. When she's ready for me to leave, I will. In the meantime, she needs the help, and I like working for her." And if she could find another job that paid as well, she would leave in a heartbeat. Being around Trace was harder than she'd ever imagined. "And I'd appreciate it if you didn't do that again." She wiped the back of her hand over her still tingling lips.

"Do what?" he asked, his blue eyes smoldering as he stared down at her.

"You know damn well what."

"You mean kiss the ranch hand?" The corners of his mouth quirked upward.

"I mean it." She lifted her chin, praying her lip didn't tremble. She'd never felt as unsteady and out of control as she did at that moment. "Don't do it again."

He stared at her for a long time and then dipped his head in the hint of a nod. "Okay. I won't kiss you… unless…"

"No unless."

He held up his hand. "I won't kiss you, unless you ask me to."

She snorted. "Good. I won't be asking."

"Uh-huh."

"I won't."

He gripped her arms and drew her close. "You won't?" he asked, his mouth so close she could feel his warm breath across hers.

Once again, air lodged in her lungs and she waited for him to claim her mouth.

As if of its own accord, her head tilted upward to receive his kiss.

The sound of a horn honking shocked Lily out of the trance Trace seemed to put her in. He glanced toward the barn door, a frown creasing his brow.

Another honk sounded.

Trace cursed. "We're not done with this conversation."

"Yes. We. Are." When Lily pushed away, Trace released her.

Her knees wobbled and her breathing seemed to

come in shallow gasps, but she was free of his hold on her.

At least his physical hold. Damn the man to hell. He still had a hold on her heart, and that would never do.

TRACE LEFT LILY and emerged from the barn to find a shiny charcoal-gray truck parked beside his black four-wheel-drive pickup.

A man had dropped down to the ground on the other side of the open driver's door.

When he closed it, he looked around and grinned when he saw Trace.

"Trace, you old son of a gun."

"Irish." Trace hurried toward his friend and former Delta Force teammate. "I thought you'd be recuperating for another couple of weeks."

"Seems I'll live after all. The doctors treated my wounds and scanned my head."

"And?"

"Concussion, a few shrapnel wounds, but nothing life-threatening. I was released once I got the all clear from the docs. Then you said you were in need of help." Irish shrugged and winced. He rolled his shoulder and held on to his middle. "So, here I am."

"I need ranch hands who can work hard. You're not up to that yet."

"But I will be within a few weeks. In the meantime, I can still handle a weapon, and I brought my own." He reached into the back seat of the truck and pulled out a gun case. "I have my own AR-15 military-grade rifle, a 9mm Glock and night vision goggles."

"What kind of help did you hear I needed?"

Irish stood in front of Trace, meeting his gaze

straight on. "I heard you needed combat veterans to help with the ranch work and protect your family from whoever killed your father."

Trace hated that he even had to call on old friends to help manage the family ranch. His father had run the operation for so many years without much problem. What had changed so drastically that they'd come to this?

"Well?" Irish raised an eyebrow. "Can you use someone like me? I like to think I'm good with animals and you know my combat skills."

Trace held up a hand. "Stop. You know you're hired. But more than that, it's good to see you're all right." He pulled Irish into a bear hug, squeezing him tightly.

"Hey, not so hard," Irish said through gritted teeth. "Injured man here."

With a chuckle, Trace released his friend and stepped back. "Just what exactly can you do right now? Can you haul hay?"

Irish cringed. "As long as I don't reopen my wounds, I can do just about anything."

Trace frowned. "We'll take it easy the first couple of weeks. I can put you to work driving the truck we'll use to haul the trailer full of bales."

"Let me see what I can do with the bales. I bet I can toss a few, no problem."

"Yeah, I bet you can. Then you'll rip a stitch and bleed everywhere. I've seen enough blood to last a lifetime. You can drive the bailing machine."

"When do you want to start?" Irish asked.

"I'd hoped to start tomorrow."

"Sounds good. Who else do you have helping?" Irish glanced around the barnyard. He nodded toward the barn. "Wow. You didn't tell me about the great scenery you had on the ranch. Please tell me she's your sister."

Trace stiffened and turned to find Lily leading the mare out to the paddock, her blue chambray shirt unbuttoned enough to display a significant amount of her cleavage and the shirttails tied in a knot around her waist, displaying her slim midriff.

He cursed beneath his breath. "I'm an only child."

Irish shot a glance toward Trace. "She with you?"

Trace snorted. "No." Then he saw the smile lighting his friend's face as he turned toward Lily. "But she's off-limits," Trace added.

The smile faded as Irish looked back at Trace. "Is she married?"

"No." His lips firming, Trace continued. "She works for my mother."

"She works for your mother, and she's off-limits." Irish shook his head. "Okay." He smiled. "You sure you're not interested in her?"

His jaw tightened as he forced out the words, "I'm sure."

"Well, it wouldn't hurt to get to know her, since she works on the ranch, too. Are you going to introduce me?"

Trace didn't want to introduce Irish to Lily. Irish had a reputation with the ladies. And he'd been pretty open about why he was getting out of the military. He wanted a real life with a real job and eventually a wife and family.

The thought of Irish flirting with Lily made Trace's gut clench.

Why was he getting wrapped around the axels about Lily? She wasn't his to claim. She'd made that perfectly clear eleven years ago when she'd chosen Matt Hennessey over him. What had happened between the two of them, he didn't know. But he intended to find out.

His best source for information might be the one closest to him.

His mother.

So many people had been to the ranch before, during and after the funeral that Trace had been hard-pressed to keep an eye on her, the ranch and Lily. The people of Whiskey Gulch had come out in force when the richest man in the area had been laid to rest. Women had shown up with food, groceries and their condolences.

His mother had stood stoically at the funeral home, receiving the guests with a warm hug and an occasional smile when someone mentioned an anecdote about his father.

Trace had stood by her, listening to how much the people had admired his father, some of the charitable actions he'd performed to help out a rancher when he was down, or a business owner who needed a loan to keep going until he could get on his feet.

Who was this man they all knew, and he didn't? His father had done things without any fanfare or expectations of undying gratitude. He'd been kind to people.

Trace had been happy to be a man on his own, making his way through life on his own terms. When he was home, he'd helped with the chores and run errands without being asked. Eventually, when they were seated at the dinner table, just the three of them and sometimes the new foreman, Roy, talk had always turned to the business of running Whiskey Gulch Ranch. Trace had refused to get caught up in his father's narrative about how he should quit the military and come home to work the ranch. His father had never accepted that he was happy with his choice to remain in the army. Never once did he say he was proud of the fact Trace had made it into the elite Delta Force. Trace tried to tell himself that he didn't care. But just once, he would have liked some acknowledgment that his father didn't think of him as a complete loser.

His mother stepped out of the house, shaded her eyes and looked their way. When she spotted Trace and Irish, she hurried out to the barnyard to greet their guest.

Lily had released Lady into the pasture and was on her way back to the barn when Trace's mother called out to her, "Lily, do you have a minute?"

Lily picked up her pace and fell into step beside Trace's mother. They spoke quietly as they closed the distance between them and Trace.

When she stopped in front of Trace and Irish, his mother gave Irish a broad grin and held out her hand. "Hi, I'm Rosalynn Travis."

Irish took her hand. "Joseph Monahan, but my friends call me Irish." He squeezed her hand gently. "I'm so sorry for your loss, ma'am."

Trace's mother gave a weak smile. "Thank you." She squared her shoulders and lifted her chin as she always did when she was being brave. "Are you a new ranch hand or a friend of Trace's?"

"Both," Trace said. "Irish is from my unit. He's coming to work for you at Whiskey Gulch Ranch, if you're okay with it."

Rosalynn frowned. "Of course I'm okay with it. You can hire all the ranch hands you want. We need the help. Our foreman should be back soon. Even then, he will be hobbling on his broken foot for a while." She turned to Lily. "Lily and I had been holding down the fort. We're so glad Trace is home and taking up the reins. Have you met Lily?" She smiled.

"No, ma'am, I haven't." Irish held out his hand to Lily.

Lily smiled at him and took his outstretched hand. "Glad to meet you."

Trace's chest tightened. She used to smile at him like that. For years, he'd wondered where he'd gone wrong with Lily. Why had she been so into him one day and then ditched him for the town bad boy?

Irish grinned. "I'd have given up the army a lot sooner if I'd known Texas was hiding some of the prettiest ranch hands in the country."

Lily's cheeks flushed a pretty pink.

His mother laughed and waved a hand at Irish. "If you were my son, I'd ask you what you were up to."

Irish winked at her. "And I'd say I only want the pleasure of your company."

His mother chuckled. "Well played."

Trace groaned. "If we could pull our feet out of the horse manure being spread so thickly on the ground, we might get some work done this afternoon."

His mother patted his cheek. "Don't be such a grouchy bear. I like your choice of a ranch hand. Irish will fit in quite well." She smiled at the man, slipped her arm through his and started toward the barn. "Come on, I'll show you where everything is. And until we get the bunkhouse cleaned up, you can stay at the house."

"Thank you, ma'am," Irish said as he left Trace staring after him, shaking his head.

"Son of a gun," Trace said beneath his breath.

"Did you warn Irish that we've had some threats here

at the ranch?" Lily asked, her gaze following Irish and Trace's mother as they entered the barn. "He's holding his side like he is nursing a wound. Is he up to the rigors of the job and the potential of being a target?"

"Irish knows what's happening here. I gave him the details when I asked him to come," Trace said. "He was injured recently, but he's on the mend. He'll be pulling light duty until he's back to one hundred percent."

"Until then, it's still me and you." Lily's lips pressed together.

"His injury isn't going to affect his ability to shoot." Trace met her gaze dead-on. "And I expect one more recruit in the next day or two."

"Your mother thinks we need to cut the hay tomorrow. Are we ready?"

Trace nodded. "Ready or not, we have to get it done. There's a storm across the Baja Peninsula predicted to come this way in less than a week. We have to have that hay cut, baled and stored before it hits."

"I'm not as worried about the round bales, but you and I are going to be hard-pressed to get the square bales packed into the barn in that short a time frame."

"Hopefully, my guy Beck will be here before we start that hay hauling. He had some commitments in San Antonio to wrap up before he could come out to help. I'm not sure he'll stay for long, and he's never worked on a ranch, but he's strong, smart and loyal. And he's prior Delta Force. He'll be a good asset to have in case we have trouble. In the meantime, we'll mow, rake and bale."

Lily nodded. "Good." She started to walk away.

"Lily, about what happened…"

She stopped and held up a hand without turning. "Already forgotten."

"That's not what I was going to say." Trace closed the distance between them. He touched her arm and turned her to face him.

"Don't—" Lily said.

He couldn't help it. He couldn't forget. "When I kissed you…"

She was already shaking her head.

He continued. "When I kissed you, you felt it, too… didn't you?"

"I don't want to talk about it." She looked up at him and then looked away.

"What happened between you and Matt?" he persisted.

"That was so long ago. Why bring it up now?" When she pulled away, he released his hold on her. "I have work to do."

"We're not finished discussing this."

"We're finished. We have nothing left to say."

"We do," he said. "And we will. Sooner or later. I'd prefer sooner. And if you don't tell me what happened between you and Matt, I'll just ask him."

Her head shot up, her eyes wide for a second before she hooded them. "He will say there never was anything between us."

"You said you were going to marry him. How could there be nothing between you two?"

She shrugged. "Maybe I changed my mind. Maybe I read too much into the relationship. Whatever it was, it didn't work out. It wasn't his fault. He wasn't the right guy for me."

Trace pressed his lips together. "Neither was I."

"It was a long time ago." She shook her head. "Let it lie." This time when she turned and walked away, he let her go.

The entire conversation left him with more questions than answers. He felt as if Lily wasn't telling him the whole truth. What was she hiding? Had she been in love with Matt? Had he dumped her? What had happened to drive them apart?

What did it matter? Lily had made it perfectly clear eleven years ago. She didn't want him then and she didn't want him now.

Then what the hell had happened when he'd kissed her? Because, though he might be rusty and maybe a little deluded, she sure as hell had kissed him back.

Chapter Five

Lily spent the rest of the day helping Irish find his way around the ranch. After Rosalynn had left him in her care, she'd shown him where the feed was stored, what and how much to feed the animals, and where the tack was stored.

"If anything is too heavy or awkward for you to lift," Lily said, "just let me know. I can help."

"I can handle this," he assured her.

Lily watched him out of the corner of her eye. He'd clutched his side occasionally when he lifted anything over twenty pounds. They had been scooping feed from the feed bins that afternoon when he clutched his side and grunted.

"Look," Lily said, "I'd rather you take time to heal. If you rip stitches now, it'll take longer for you to mend. I'll handle the hay bales, you can feed the horses, pigs and chickens."

"I can do more than that," Irish insisted and bent to lift a scoop full of sweet feed out of the bin.

She chuckled. "Oh, you will. We need to check the fences around the property. There's always some that need mending. What can you do? What do you have experience with?"

"I was a sniper in the Delta Force."

"Ever worked on a ranch?" she asked, not sure this man who'd been injured would be an asset even after he recovered fully.

"I did, one summer when I was in high school." He gave her a weak smile. "Does that count?"

She carried a bucket full of grain to one of the horse stalls and hung it inside the pen, then turned. "Did you work with the animals?"

Irish carried another bucket over to the adjacent stall and hung it inside. "I was in charge of hooking the horses up to walkers, cleaning hooves, currying, feeding and exercising them. I also helped corral the cattle to administer worm medication. Not to mention hauling hay, mending fences and anything else that came up."

"All in one summer?" she asked.

He nodded. "I wasn't raised on a farm, but I loved working with animals." He looked over the stall door at the horse happily munching on the feed. "When I processed out of the military, I wanted to get back to working with animals."

"Well, Mr. Monahan, you're back. Be ready for some hard, dirty and altogether rewarding work." Lily smiled. "I wasn't raised on a ranch, either. I learned as I went. If you aren't afraid of hard work, you'll do well here."

"I'm ex–Delta Force," he said, puffing out his chest. "I didn't get there by being lazy."

Lily nodded. "I can see why Trace brought you on board."

"That, and I'm good with a variety of weapons." Irish frowned. "Trace gave me a brief synopsis of what's been happening around here. I was sorry to hear about his father. Has the local law enforcement come up with any indication as to who was responsible?"

Lily shook her head. "He was alone when it happened. No witnesses. The other ranch hands were working together on another part of the ranch. They weren't anywhere near Mr. Travis. Our foreman had gone to town for supplies. No one from the Whiskey Gulch Ranch was anywhere near Mr. Travis when he was shot."

"Did they question the neighbors?" he asked.

"They did." Lily nodded. "They all had alibis."

"Figures." Irish returned to the feed bin for another bucket of feed.

"What about you?" Lily asked. "Why did you decide to get out of the military? Or did you have to get out because of your injuries?"

He chuckled. "My team was mystified as well." He tapped his torso. "The injuries weren't life-threatening. Yeah, I had a concussion, but thankfully, it doesn't appear to be a traumatic brain injury. And I've had worse shrapnel wounds." He carried the bucket to another stall. "I've been deployed so many times, I don't remember where I live half the time. I've also watched some of my buddies get married and then get divorced. Their wives couldn't handle them being away so often. I'm in my thirties and, if I want a home and a family, I don't stand a chance of finding anything that would last if I stayed on active duty."

Lily chuckled. "So basically what you're telling me is that your biological clock is ticking, and you didn't want it to run out before you had a chance at having a wife and children." She touched his arm. "I don't mean to laugh. I just think it's ironic."

"What about you?" Irish raised an eyebrow. "I don't see a ring on your finger. Does that mean you aren't married? Or that you don't like to wear jewelry when you're up to your elbows in horse manure?"

Lily laughed. "Both. I'm not married. And I wouldn't wear jewelry to muck out stalls."

"How did a beautiful woman like you manage to escape the matrimonial ring?"

She shrugged. "I guess I just haven't found the right person. Or he hasn't found me." She hung her bucket in a stall and wiped her hands on her jeans. "We're done in here. We should go wash up. Mrs. Travis should have dinner on the table soon."

She led the way out of the barn and closed the door behind her.

"I've known Trace four years, and I didn't know that he was the heir to all of this." Irish waved a hand at the barn, the pastures and the massive ranch house. "He never mentioned that his family was loaded."

Lily smiled. "He never considered himself rich. It was his father's ranch, his father's money and his father's life. Trace wanted to make it on his own."

"Sounds like Trace," Irish said. "He was always so focused and driven. I guess that's why."

She nodded. "They butted heads often."

Irish shook his head. "He was just one of the guys. He never expected special favors, and he always had our backs. We could count on him."

Lily's heart pinched hard in her chest. She'd known he'd make it on his own. He was so much like his father, he couldn't have failed. They both worked hard and smart to make things happen.

"If you don't mind my asking," Irish started, "what's

up between you and Trace? I sense an undercurrent and I can't quite put my finger on it."

With a shrug, Lily picked up the pace. "There's nothing up between me and Trace. Nothing." Out of the corner of her eye, she could see Irish studying her, his eyes slightly narrowed. Lily held her breath, praying Irish didn't continue along his current line of questioning.

"I was just asking. You know…pretty, single girl on a ranch. I might want to ask you out." He winked. "But if you're spoken for, I don't want to step on anyone's toes."

"I'm single. You're not going to step on anyone's toes, but I'm not interested in dating at this time."

"Okay, then. Maybe we can just be friends?"

She smiled. "I'd like that."

He held out his hand. "Deal?"

She shook his hand. "Deal."

As she climbed the steps up to the back porch, Lily smiled.

The door to the kitchen opened and Trace came out, carrying a tray of raw steaks. He frowned when he saw her and Irish.

"You need a hand with those?" Irish asked. "I've been known to grill a mean medium rare steak."

Trace shook his head. "I've got this. You can grab a beer and keep me company, though."

Irish grinned. "Now you're speaking my language. Point me in the right direction."

Without making eye contact with Trace, Lily touched Irish's arm. "I'll show you where they keep the beer after we wash up."

"Great." Irish grinned at Trace. "Lily's been a big help clueing me in on what has to be done around here."

Trace grunted and walked by, his gaze capturing

Lily's. "I'll get these on the fire. You might check with my mother to see if there's anything else she wants to cook out here." His tone was clipped, his frown seemingly carved into his forehead.

"Got it. I'll be out in a sec." Lily dived into the house to escape Trace's piercing glance that seared straight through to her soul. Her face heated and her palms were sweating by the time she reached the downstairs bathroom.

"Are you all right?" Irish asked as she passed him to enter the washroom first.

"I'm fine. I'll be right out." She shut the door between them and stood staring at her flushed face in the mirror. Why did Trace have such a huge effect on her after all these years?

The answer was the kiss.

She should have stood her ground, turned her face, done anything rather than let him kiss her.

The truth was…she'd wanted that kiss as much as she'd wanted to take her next breath. Hell, she was in so much trouble where Trace was concerned. She wasn't over him by any stretch. The only thing she could do was stay away from him and get on with her life. The kiss had meant nothing to him but a way to prove a point. That he could still turn her willpower to mush.

After washing her hands and splashing water on her face, she felt more like herself. She exited the bathroom with a smile pinned to her face. "All yours. Think you can find your way to the kitchen when you're finished?"

"I've got a keen sense of direction," Irish said. "Which way do I go?"

She gave him directions.

He gave her a mock salute. "Got it." Irish entered the bathroom and closed the door.

Rather than go out to the porch and relax in one of the rocking chairs, Lily went straight to the kitchen. "Anything I can do to help?" she asked.

"Actually, yes." Rosalynn shot a smile over her shoulder. "You can set the table and put ice in the glasses."

Lily pulled cutlery out of the drawer and plates from one of the cabinets, enough for four people.

"We'll need an extra setting," Rosalynn said.

"Oh?"

"Yes. I've hired another man to help haul hay. He's supposed to be here any moment."

"Anyone I know?"

"I think so." Rosalynn pulled the Dutch oven full of baked beans from the oven, set it on a trivet on the table and wiped her hands on a dish towel. "I'll be right back."

Curious, Lily quickly set the table with the silverware and plates. Then she put ice in the glasses and placed a pitcher of tea in the center of the table. It felt weird and sad that Mr. Travis wasn't at the table. Before he'd passed, he'd insisted on having dinner at the formal dining table. Since his death, his widow had gone to having dinner at the large table in the kitchen.

Still, his powerful presence was missed.

Having Trace home helped. At least, it helped his mother. She'd seemed so lost without her husband. Sure, she'd taken up the reins of running the ranch even though she'd been devastated, but when she'd learned that the foreman had run off the road and crushed his foot the same day, Lily thought Rosalynn would fall the rest of the way apart.

But she hadn't. Not even when the ranch hands had each called to say they couldn't work there anymore because their families had been threatened. Rosalynn had squared her shoulders, visited Roy in the hospital briefly and gone back to take care of the ranch her husband had loved so much.

Lily had gone from being household staff to a ranch hand, doing the best she could to keep the animals fed, the barn clean and Mrs. Travis from working herself into an early grave with her husband.

She hadn't wanted to notify the Red Cross of her husband's death to bring Trace home to help.

Frankly, neither had Lily, but the situation had become impossible to handle. Either they got someone there to help, or Rosalynn would be forced to sell the ranch or at least all the animals on it. She couldn't keep up with the amount of work it took to keep it going. Not by herself. Lily had made the call to the Red Cross. She'd waited until it was too late to recall the notice to tell her. Rosalynn had been relieved. Despite her protests to the contrary, she needed to have her only son there for the funeral and to help her decide what to do next. After all, if she wanted to keep the ranch, it would eventually go to Trace.

Lily sliced lemons for the iced tea and set out the fresh salad Rosalynn had cut up, steak sauce and napkins. By the time she was finished, Irish appeared in the doorway, carrying a tray of baked potatoes wrapped in foil. A moment later, Trace appeared, carrying another tray filled with juicy steaks. The aroma filled the air, making Lily's mouth water and her tummy rumble. She hadn't realized just how hungry she was until that moment.

When her gaze met Trace's, all thoughts of hunger jumped from food to desire. She physically ached for this man, and they could never be together.

Lily took the tray of potatoes from Irish with a smile that hurt her face. "Thank you." She plucked a potato from the tray and nearly dropped it, her fingers on fire. "Ouch."

"Careful." Irish frowned. "They're fresh from the grill and hot."

Lily shook her hand, wincing in pain. "I know that… now."

Trace set his tray on the table and crossed to her. He took the platter of potatoes from her grip and set it beside the steaks. Then he gripped her wrist and studied the red mark on her fingertips. "Come on." He led her to the sink and ran her hand beneath cool water.

With Trace holding her hand and standing so close to her that his hip bumped against hers, Lily could barely breathe, much less think.

After a couple of minutes, he turned off the water and stared down at her hand again. "That might blister."

"I'll be okay," she said, her voice kind of breathy. Hardly the strong voice of a confident woman who could handle anything.

Anything but Trace.

"Oh, good, I'm glad everyone is ready to eat," Rosalynn said from the entrance to the kitchen. "I want you all to welcome our guest."

Lily turned a split second after Trace did.

His fingers tightened around her wrist.

Lily felt the blood drain from her face when she spied the man following Rosalynn.

"Most of you know Matt Hennessey," Rosalynn started, "am I right?"

"Yes. The question is, what the hell is he doing here?" Trace demanded.

Mrs. Travis frowned at Trace and smiled up at Matt. "He's agreed to help us bring in the hay and whatever else needs to be done. At least until we can hire full-time staff to do the work."

"We don't need help," Trace bit out. "Especially from him."

"Now, Trace, Matt is our guest," Rosalynn said.

"He doesn't belong here," Trace said.

His mother lifted her chin and met his stare with one of her own. "You said it yourself, it's my home and I will decide who stays and who goes."

Lily could almost hear the sound of Trace's teeth grinding together. The tension in the air was so tightly strung, Lily could easily feel it plucking at her nerves.

Matt stood with a half smile tugging at one corner of his mouth. "Told you it wasn't a good idea." He turned. "I'll just be leaving."

Mrs. Travis grabbed his arm, her chin lifting, her mouth pressing into a thin line. "This is still my house, and I'll invite whoever I want to the dinner table. *And* I'll hire whoever I want to help bring in the hay. Matt has so graciously offered to take time away from his own business to help us get the hay in before it rains. I don't expect you to smile, but you *will* say thank you. No one else in town has offered to help. The animals depend on us to provide feed throughout the winter. Now, if you'll excuse me, I have a pasta salad in the refrigerator." She jerked her head toward the table. "Please, Matt, have a seat. Dinner is served."

His half smile became a grin. "Thank you, ma'am. I haven't had a home-cooked meal in a while."

"Well, you'll have one tonight. My son grilled the steaks and potatoes. You know Trace and Lily." She reached into the refrigerator for a large bowl and straightened. "Irish is the new ranch hand. He's a friend of Trace's from the military."

Irish held out his hand. "Joseph Monahan, but you can call me Irish. I'm fresh off active duty."

Matt shook Irish's hand. "Army?"

Irish nodded. "Ten years."

Matt tipped his head. "I did seven years in the Marine Corps."

"Deploy?"

Matt's lips thinned. "A number of times. Would have stayed, but a bullet ruined my knee. Uncle Sam kindly asked me to retire."

"Matt owns an engine repair shop in town." Mrs. Travis set a pasta salad on the table. "We'll only have him until the hay is harvested and stored."

"Thank you, Matt," Lily said softly, her pulse hammering so hard in her veins she could hear it thumping in her ears. She couldn't think of a worse situation.

How was she going to endure sitting at the table with the man she loved and the one he thought she'd ditched him for?

She supposed karma had a large part in the circumstances. Some lies seemed to have a life of their own.

Chapter Six

Trace sat at the opposite end of the table from his mother with a clear view of the man he'd hated for eleven years sitting as pretty as he pleased across the table from the woman he'd loved all those years ago.

He guessed he deserved it for holding on to those feelings for so long, letting them define his life and relationships. If he'd let go long ago, he might have found someone else to love even more than his high school sweetheart. Instead, his love hadn't faded but morphed into a wound that festered and fed darkness into his soul.

"I ran into Matt today at the grocery store. When he offered to help me in any way he could, I don't think he expected me to take him up on his offer." Trace's mother smiled as she scooped pasta salad onto her plate and passed the bowl to the left.

Trace stabbed a steak with his fork and dropped it onto his plate. What he didn't understand was how easily Lily sat across from Matt without glaring at him or kicking him beneath the table. He would have expected her to be a little less generous toward the man who'd promised to marry her and then dumped her. Was the man insane? Trace would have held on to her with everything in his power.

Then why hadn't he tried to change her mind?

He had been so hurt, he'd buried himself in his new life in the army, working harder than anyone. The more he pushed, the less time he had to mourn the loss of Lily's love. He'd pushed so hard and so fast, he'd caught the attention of his drill sergeant, who recommended him for further training that eventually led him to the army rangers and selection into the elite Delta Force.

Irish took a steak off the platter and passed it to Lily.

"I'd heard the rumors around town that you were having trouble keeping help after Mr. Travis's death." Matt peeled the foil off a baked potato and cut it down the middle. "He was a good man. He helped me get a start with my shop when the banks wouldn't loan me the money to buy the building."

Trace had been at loggerheads with his father for so many years, he hadn't known his father had helped other people in the community from time to time. But Hennessey? What a cruel trick of fate that his father had helped the one man who'd taken the only woman his son had ever loved away from him.

Now his mother was fawning over the guy in front of him. Yeah, fate was cruel.

"I still owe half of what he loaned to me a year ago," Matt said. "I promise to pay it off as soon as I can."

"I'm not worried about the money," his mother said. "I know you're good for it."

Trace would have to pull his mother aside and warn her about being too nice. People would take advantage of her, thinking she was a pushover.

"We need to start cutting hay tomorrow afternoon," his mother said with a smile.

"Why not in the morning first thing?" Trace asked.

His mother looked down at her plate, her smile fading. "We have a meeting at the attorney's office to go over your father's will." She glanced up, her gaze going to Lily and Matt. "The attorney asked that Lily and Matt be present for the reading."

Trace felt anger rise up inside him. "Why? I thought Dad would leave everything to you."

His mother set her fork beside her plate and folded her hands in her lap. "Don't worry. He took care of me. But he wanted to be certain others were taken care of as well, if he should pass before I did."

"I don't understand," Trace said. "You were his wife. You have every right to all of his estate."

"Just so you all know, I was with him when he put the provisions into the will. I signed it as well. I'm aware of everything the lawyer is going to say tomorrow."

"Then why don't you tell us now?" Trace demanded.

"I think you need to hear what the attorney has to say first, then I'll tell you why your father and I did what we did." She lifted her fork.

When Trace opened his mouth, his mother gave him *that look* that meant the discussion was over.

He bit down hard on his tongue to keep from shouting.

Not only had the man stolen his girl, but Matt had also wormed his way into his father's good graces and somehow stolen money from his family. Trace didn't want his father's money, but he sure as hell didn't want Matt Hennessey to have a single dime.

Lily reached out to touch Trace's mother's hand.

His mother glanced up at her and gave her a watery smile.

That exchange of silent communication reminded Trace that his mother had just lost the man she'd centered her life around. They'd been married for more than thirty-five years. Most of their lives had been spent together.

His anger was uncalled for in the wake of her loss.

Despite his differences with his father, he'd loved the man. His father had been the one who'd taught him the important things in life. Like how to ride a horse, how to throw a baseball and football, and how to love a woman.

James Travis had been a force to be reckoned with. His concern for his son came from the heart. He'd wanted the best for his son. That didn't include marrying a woman whose parents were a prostitute and a thief. He'd probably thought he was giving Trace good advice. What he didn't know was that Trace wasn't a kid anymore. He could make his own decisions, and he resented his father's interference in making those decisions. His father hadn't understood that Trace needed to be the master of his own destiny, to make his own mistakes and follow his heart where it led.

Based on the way things had turned out, his father might have been half right. Trace had decided he wanted Lily. Lily had made the decision for him that he wouldn't have her. His father might have seen that coming and tried to spare him the heartache.

That wouldn't have changed Trace's mind about joining the army. He'd have done it anyway. He was glad he had. For the first time in his life, he was his own person. Not the son of the richest man in the county. And he'd done well for himself. If not financially, then for his own state of mind.

Irish broke the silence with "What's in this pasta salad, Mrs. Travis? It's really good."

Trace's mother smiled, the lines of tension easing from her face. Soon, Irish had the others laughing over stories about his antics as a young recruit going through basic training.

Before long, the meal was over. The steak Trace had eaten sat like a rock in the pit of his belly. What had his father left in his will for Matt and Lily? And why them? Did he know they were once a couple? That they were responsible for breaking his son's heart?

Trace carried his plate to the sink.

"I'll pull KP," Irish said.

"No, I've got this," his mother said.

"Seriously, you've been working as hard as anyone," Irish said. "You need to relax and go watch that sunset I can see through the window."

Trace's mother filled the sink with soapy water. "If we all pitch in, we can get it done faster and then we can all see that sunset." She handed Irish a dry dish towel. "I'll wash, you dry, Lily and Trace can put the dishes away, and Matt can open a bottle of wine and pour me a glass."

With tasks assigned, they worked together to get the dishes done in record time.

Once they had everything put away, they adjourned to the porch to watch the brilliant orange-and-mauve-painted sky as the sun sank below the horizon.

Matt leaned against the porch rail, staring out at the

last rays as they disappeared. "This place is amazing. Don't let anyone take it away from you."

"We have no intention of letting that happen," his mother said. "It's been in the Travis family for more than a hundred years. But it's not the life everyone would choose."

Trace tensed. He knew she was talking about him. Before he left for the army, one of his last arguments with his father had been over the ranch and who would inherit it. He'd told his father that he didn't care who he left the ranch to. But, good Lord, not Matt Hennessey.

LILY SAT ON the porch swing beside Irish, talking quietly about life in the little Texas town of Whiskey Gulch. Irish asked questions and she answered but didn't go into the details of how she'd been ostracized by most of her peers growing up because of who her parents were. She didn't tell him that she'd been bullied and picked on by the mean girls and propositioned by just about every male in the county who thought she was like her mother.

Trace had been one of a handful of people who hadn't been mean to her. He'd seen her for who she was, not who her parents were.

When Irish excused himself and went inside, Trace gathered the empty beer bottles and carried them into the house.

Lily stood and stretched. "I'm going to check on the barn cat. I think she's expecting to drop a litter of kittens soon. I want to make sure she's okay. I might need to relocate the kittens if she's had them up in the loft, since we'll be filling that space soon."

"I'll go with you," Rosalynn said.

"No need," Lily said. "I'll only be a minute. I'm sure she's fine."

"We'll need to catch her and get her and all the kittens spayed or neutered before we end up with a couple dozen cats around here. But that'll be after the kittens are weaned." Rosalynn settled back in her rocking chair. "If you're sure you don't need me, I'll just sit here and listen to the cicadas sing. James loved the sound. I always thought they were loud." She smiled. "I miss him."

Lily touched her shoulder. "I miss him, too."

Rosalynn covered her hand on her shoulder. "Thank you for being here for me, Lily. I don't know what I'd have done without you."

"I haven't done anything anyone else wouldn't have. I'm glad I was here for you." She leaned down and pressed a kiss to the top of Rosalynn's head. "I'll be back in a minute."

Lily left the porch and strolled out to the barn. After the tension of dinner and being in the same space as Trace and Matt for an extended period of time, she needed to get away from the house, from Trace and from her own thoughts.

The mama cat would do fine birthing her kittens. She didn't need Lily to help her along, but it had been a good excuse for her to step away for a few minutes by herself.

Lily entered the barn and flipped the switch on the wall. The lights blinked on, giving the interior a soft yellow glow.

Several soft whinnies greeted her.

Lily chuckled. "You've already been fed."

Lady stomped her foot impatiently.

She reached over the stall door and rubbed the mare's nose. "Your hooves must be feeling better if you're doing that."

A sound near the back of the barn caught her attention. She squinted, trying to see into the shadows. "Patches, is that you, girl?" Lily stepped toward the sound.

Lady stomped louder, her hoof hitting the wooden wall, making a loud banging sound.

"It's okay," Lily said and reached back to pat the horse.

A shiver rippled across Lily's skin. The day had been hot, but with the setting of the sun, the warmth disappeared, and the night had cooled at least fifteen degrees.

Rubbing her arms, Lily searched the corners and shadows for the mama cat.

The animal wasn't behind the feed bins or nestled in the stacks of empty feed sacks. The tack room door was kept closed to keep her out. Had someone inadvertently locked her inside?

Lily pushed the door to the tack room open and peered inside. "Patches?" she called out. When she started to turn around, she caught movement in her peripheral vision. Before she could duck or move out of the way, something dark swung toward her and hit her on the side of her head, knocking her to the ground.

She lay stunned, her vision blurred, her head spinning and pain knifing through her temple. How long she lay there, she didn't know until someone stepped into the doorway. With the yellow lighting behind him, he appeared a dark, shadowy figure.

Lily whimpered and tried to scramble away from

him. "Don't," she said and raised her hand to shield her face.

"Lily?" a voice said as if from a distance. Then the figure squatted down beside her and she could see his familiar face.

Trace.

When he reached for her, she fell into his arms.

"It's okay," he murmured. "It's okay." He smoothed his hand over her hair.

For a moment, she let him hold her. "No." She pushed away from him, frantically trying to get around him to see what was on the other side of his hulking body.

"What?" Trace asked.

"He might get you." Lily shook her head, trying to clear the fog. It hurt, but she couldn't be deterred.

"Who might?" Trace rose and helped her to her feet. "What are you talking about?"

"He might hit you." She pushed him to the side and stood in front of him.

"He who?" Trace gripped her arm. "Lily, why were you lying on the floor?"

"Someone hit me," she said.

Immediately, Trace shoved her into the tack room. "Stay here and don't unlock the door until I tell you to. Promise?"

Fear gripped her. Not for herself, but for Trace. "What are you going to do?"

"I'm going to find whoever is in the barn." He closed the door. "Lock it," he said from the other side.

"What about you?" she asked, her voice shaking.

"I'll be all right." He paused as if waiting for her to comply. When she didn't, he said, "Lily, lock the damn door."

Lily turned the lock and waited on the other side, her ear pressed to the wood, listening and praying Trace would be okay.

For what felt like an eternity, she held her breath.

"You can unlock the door," Trace's voice said from the other side. "Whoever was here is gone."

Lily twisted the lock, ripped open the door and flung herself into his arms. "Thank God... I was afraid..."

He held her until she stopped shaking, smoothing the hair at the back of her neck. After a while, he leaned back and stared into her face. "Where did he hit you?"

She touched her fingertips to her temple and winced. "Here."

He tipped her head to the side to allow the light to shine down on her face. "You have a small cut that will likely boast a bruise by morning. Let's get you into the house and put something on it."

Lily stepped out of the tack room, shaking her head. "Who was in here?"

Trace's jaw was tight, and his eyes narrowed. "I don't know. I don't like it. From now on, no one ventures out at night or any other time alone. We have to have a buddy system." He cupped her elbow and guided her toward the barn door.

Lily dug her heels in, bringing them to a halt. "Patches."

Trace frowned. "Patches?"

"The mama cat who lives in the barn. She's due to have kittens anytime. I came out here to check on her."

"She'll know what to do when the time comes. Let's get you inside and take care of your wound." Again, he tried to guide her to the door.

She pulled free of his grip. "You can go ahead. I'm

not going until I know where she is. If she's hidden in the loft, we could trap her in when we stack the hay." Lily strode toward the stairs leading up into the loft.

"Wait." Trace caught her around the waist as she started up the stairs and swung her back to the ground. "If anyone is going up, it's me."

She tipped her head. "If you go up, that leaves me alone on the ground."

His lips twisted. "You've got a point. Okay. I'll go up first in case your attacker is hiding up there. You come right after me."

Lily didn't like the idea that the attacker might still be in the barn, waiting for one of them to climb up into the loft. Nor did she like the idea that Trace was going up first and could be coldcocked like she'd been. However, he was bigger, better trained in combat skills and pretty darn intimidating.

"Okay," she said.

Trace grabbed a riding whip from a hook on the wall and started up the stairs.

The bulb hanging from the ceiling gave just enough light for them to see the loft, except in the far corners where several stacks of last year's hay stood, three bales high.

Trace edged his way across the wooden floor to a stack of hay, holding the riding whip in front of him. "Remind me to start carrying my Glock."

"Start carrying your Glock," Lily whispered.

He snorted. "Remind me when I'm still in the house." Slowly, he circled the short stack of hay until he stood to the side and could see behind it. The shadow hid anything below the top bale.

Lily pulled her cell phone out of her back pocket, turned on the flashlight feature and shined it down the back of the bales.

The light reflected off a pair of red orbs.

"Patches!" Lily brushed past Trace and knelt beside the gray-and-white cat.

The mama cat had given birth to five kittens in varying shades of gray, white and wheat gold.

"Look at you," Lily cooed. "Five pretty babies and you found a nice warm and dry place to have them." She studied the kittens, all tiny creatures, their eyes closed, struggling to find purchase at one of their mother's teats.

"We need to move her before we stack the hay in here," Lily said.

"If we move her, she could move them back," Trace argued. "She probably had them here because she felt safe."

"True." Lily touched a finger to her chin and looked around the loft and over the railing to the barn below. "Where would she be safe and not feel like she had to move them again?"

"I don't know. But let's leave them here for now. We probably won't stack hay for a couple of days. We'll cut tomorrow, let it dry and then rake and bale. When we get close to hauling the hay, we can relocate her to the tack room until we're finished."

Lily nodded. "That would be best." She smiled down at the tiny kittens crawling across Patches's belly instinctively looking for something to eat.

When she pushed to her feet, she swayed a little.

Trace reached out and pulled her into his arms. "I

shouldn't have let you come up here when you've had a head injury." He brushed her hair away from her temple and stared at the wound. "Let's get you back to the house."

"Yes. I'm worried about your mother. She was sitting alone on the porch."

"She was going in for the night when I stepped out of the house." He walked her to the stairs leading downward. "Need help getting down?"

Lily shook her head. "No. I got up on my own. I can get down on my own."

His lips quirked. "Always were independent."

She tipped her chin upward. "You used to like that about me."

His gaze shifted from her eyes to her lips. "There were a lot of things I liked about you."

Lily's heart beat a rapid tattoo against her ribs.

Trace stood so close, she could reach out and touch him. If she stood on her toes, she could press her lips to his and kiss him. Lily swayed toward him, caught herself up before she lost her mind and lurched toward the stairs.

Trace took her wrist and pulled her back. "Me first."

Lily held back, letting him descend to the ground, giving her a little more time to pull herself together. Had he felt that tug of desire, that longing for more than just words? He'd kissed her earlier that day. Had it meant anything to him?

It meant something to her. It meant all those years of trying to forget him had been a waste of time. Trace had been and always would be the only man she would ever love. When the time came, she'd have to leave. She couldn't stay around to see him fall in love and marry another woman. That would wreck her, shatter her into a million pieces.

She couldn't let that happen. If it meant leaving Whiskey Gulch Ranch and her hometown, so be it.

Chapter Seven

After the sheriff's deputy had come to investigate the attack in the barn, looked around and taken Lily's statement, Trace went around the house, checking windows and doors to make sure all had been securely locked.

His mother had doctored the wound on Lily's face.

Irish, having been trained as one of the medics on the Delta Force team, had checked Lily's pupils for possibility of concussion.

When he'd suggested she see a doctor, Lily had promptly refused, claiming she hadn't been knocked unconscious and she was feeling much better. Irish then offered to check on her throughout the night to make sure she didn't show any signs of complications. Again, Lily had thanked him but politely refused.

Trace spent the night tossing and turning. Sleep eluded him. Worried about Lily, he'd listened for sounds through the wall between their rooms. At one point, he'd left his bed, tiptoed out into the hallway and tried the door to her room.

It had been unlocked. Feeling a little guilty, he'd stepped inside and checked to make sure she was breathing. For a few long moments, he'd stood beside her bed until he saw the reassuring rise and fall of her chest beneath the sheets. Relieved, he'd wanted more than anything to kiss Lily and hold her like he had when they were younger.

Unfortunately, they were no longer hormonal teens. They had matured into adults and gone their separate ways. Only now those ways had converged.

When he'd left his unit, he hadn't thought far enough ahead of getting home to know where his future would lead. Now that he was back on the Whiskey Gulch Ranch, he couldn't imagine going back to his unit and leaving his mother with only the help of their foreman and Lily to manage the ranch on their own.

If his mother planned to stay, he'd have to stay as well. If she wanted to sell the ranch, he couldn't stop her. As far as he knew, she would inherit his father's ranch and had the authority to do whatever she wanted with it.

As he worked in the barn, in the fields and around the house, he remembered growing up with the world at his feet. His father had demanded that he work hard, but he always had chances to play hard as well.

Many summer afternoons, he'd ridden horses with his friends across the pastures to the creek, where they would swim and lie in the sun until dusk.

Lily had been with him on many of those occasions. That was how he'd started to fall in love with her in the first place. She'd been his friend before she'd been his lover. She'd been his first love. They'd picnicked by the creek, chased squirrels and lain in the back of his truck to witness the shooting stars in a heaven full of diamonds. The most beautiful stars were those reflected in Lily's eyes.

He'd been so in love with her that when she'd broken up with him, it had hit him like a physical blow. He had not seen it coming.

Now that he was back, and she was underfoot, he couldn't avoid her or the feelings that had resurfaced after all these years.

Rather than disturb her sleep, he'd left her room, returned to his and lain on top of the covers, willing sleep to take him.

It hadn't.

Unwilling to wait for morning to dawn, he'd left his bed, dressed and gone out to the barn as the sun edged up over the horizon.

"You're up early," a voice called out to him from the open door of the barn. Irish stood in the sunshine, wearing a clean gray T-shirt and jeans. "Couldn't sleep?"

"No." He stacked a saddle on a saddle tree, adjusting the stirrups to hang free on either side.

He'd spent the morning cleaning and rearranging the tack room. With Roy out of commission for the time being, he could get in, assess and decide what needed to stay and what could go. Roy had a tendency to hoard everything, even long after its expiration date or usefulness. Trace made a list of supplies he needed, from horse feed to wormer, fence nails to new curry combs and brushes.

"Worried about your father's will?" Irish grabbed a broom and swept dust and straw out of the far corner of the tack room.

Trace hadn't really thought about his father's will. He'd been too busy thinking about Lily and how much he'd wanted to kiss her. Now that Irish had reminded him of the will, he might actually shift his obsession from her to whatever his father had done with his holdings. "My father owned the ranch. He and my mother have every right to do with it whatever they want."

Irish's brow rose. "You don't want a part of it?"

"Not if they don't want me to have it," Trace said.

"Would be a shame for it to go out of the family."

"Ranching is hard work," Trace said. "My father and his father before him built this place to what it is today with their own sweat and blood."

Irish snorted. "And you didn't help them in their efforts?"

"Not as much as my father would have liked." His father had always found fault with his work, no matter how much effort he put into it.

"He wanted you to stay and run it, didn't he?" Irish guessed.

Trace didn't respond.

"This place is amazing." Irish waved a hand around the interior of the barn. "Why would you want to join the army and barely make a living when you had all this?"

Anger bubbled up inside Trace. "Because it wasn't mine, and I had no say in how it should be run. If I'd stayed, my father would have continued to run Whiskey Gulch Ranch the way he saw fit. He didn't trust me to make any of the decisions. And why should he? I'd never had to be responsible for anything as long as he was in charge."

Irish nodded. "I get that."

Trace looped a bridle over a peg on the wall and faced Irish. "Yeah, well, he didn't. You ready for breakfast?" He headed out of the barn and strode toward the house. The scent of bacon made his stomach rumble. Although he was hungry, his gut was knotted in anticipation of the contents of the will. He really did care what happened to Whiskey Gulch Ranch. Like his father and his father's father before him, they were rooted in the place. Trace had left to prove to himself he could be himself, not the son of James Travis. In the back of his mind, he knew he'd eventually come home. He hadn't thought it would be for his father's funeral.

Irish fell in step beside him. "Just so you know, I don't expect to be fed and housed by you and your family."

"No worries. The ranch employs ranch hands who live here and those who don't. Most of those who don't have families and live in town. The single guys have a choice of living here or in town. We have a bunkhouse my father converted into small apartments to give the guys more personal space. It's up to you. When we have a cook, he—" Trace paused, thinking about Lily "—or she will provide a hot breakfast and dinner and the means to make a sack lunch if you want it."

"I appreciate everything you've done for me. I'd like to stay on the ranch at least until I figure out the area. I can help get the bunkhouse ready, so that I don't take up room in the big house."

"No hurry. Our main focus, after hearing what is in the will, is to get the hay in before it rains." Trace glanced up at the clear blue sky. "It is Texas, and the rain may or may not happen, but we have to be prepared."

"Got it." Irish squared his shoulders. "I'll do the best I can."

Trace clapped a hand on his friend's shoulder. "I know you will. That's why I asked you to come. I just hope you stick around. Ranching life isn't for everyone.

Especially guys like us who've been where we've been. It can be boring here. There's not always that adrenaline rush of going into battle."

"I'm looking forward to that," Irish said. "I could use a little downtime."

"Especially to give yourself time to heal." Trace gave Irish a pointed glance. "We need your help, but only as much as you can do without reinjuring yourself." Trace frowned. "Will you be all right here alone while the rest of us are in town at the lawyer's office?"

Irish nodded. "Someone has to stay here and guard the homestead. I'll be sure to keep an eye out for danger. You don't have to worry about me."

Trace climbed the porch to the big house. "Be sure to keep your weapons where you can use them."

"I'll pack my pistol when I step outside and keep my rifle handy." Irish opened the back door to the house and held it for Trace.

"Whoever is causing trouble is getting cocky and dangerously close. I don't want you having just come back from a war zone to be injured or killed stateside."

Irish gave a crooked smile. "That would be the ultimate irony."

"Yeah. Don't let it happen. Stay close to the house and be careful, my friend." He clasped Irish's hand in a firm grasp and pulled him in for a hug. "Don't make me regret asking you to come."

"Wouldn't dream of it. I owe you one for saving my butt back in Afghanistan."

"You don't owe me a thing. You've saved me more times than I can remember."

"Any idea who might be targeting the ranch?" Irish asked.

"None." Trace clenched his fists. "Whoever hit Lily in the barn got away clean. He must have come in on foot and left in a hurry."

Irish shook his head. "Why do you think he was in the barn? He couldn't have known Lily would go out after the chores were complete."

"I don't know." Trace led the way to the kitchen and the smell of bacon cooking. "We'll just have to be more vigilant."

"Who will have to be more vigilant?" his mother asked from her position at the coffee maker.

"We all will." Lily stood at the stove, pushing fluffy yellow scrambled eggs around in the pan. "Y'all ready for breakfast?" When she turned, the bruise at her temple and the cut were evident.

Trace's blood boiled all over again. If he'd caught the guy who'd hit her, he'd have pummeled him to near death.

"I'm starving," Irish said. "What can I do to help?"

"Tell me what you want to drink and have a seat," Trace's mother said. "Everything is ready and on the table except for the eggs, and Lily has that under control."

"Done." Lily scooped eggs into a large bowl and carried it to the table.

Trace couldn't help but watch her as she moved across the floor in jeans, a powder blue blouse and her cowboy boots. She had her long blond hair pulled back and secured in a ponytail at the nape of her neck. Several tendrils had worked their way loose and curled around her cheeks.

A deep, physical ache pinched his chest.

Irish held a chair for Trace's mother. "Ma'am."

She smiled at him. "Please, don't call me ma'am. It makes me feel old."

"Yes, Mrs. Travis."

Her eyes filled. "No." She drew in a deep breath and forced a bit of a smile. "Call me Rosalynn."

Trace had been so focused on Lily and his lingering feelings for her that he hadn't been nearly as attentive to his mother. He waited for her to take her seat, then sat at the opposite end of the table from her. "You all right?" he asked softly.

She met his gaze, a tear slipping down her cheek. "You look just like your father when he was in his thirties. Seeing you sometimes hurts."

"I'm sorry," he said.

She laughed, the sound catching in her throat. "You have nothing to be sorry about. I like to think he's still here, in you. You two were so much alike."

Growing up, Trace had wanted to get away from his father as fast as he could. They never saw eye to eye, and they were constantly butting heads. Back then, he'd never considered that they had similar personalities.

Now he could see what his mother had observed back then. They were both stubborn, driven, and they liked to be in control of a situation. He'd come to grips with this when he'd been in the army and performing operations with his Delta Force team. Until he'd gained enough experience, he'd had to give control to those who'd been at it longer and knew the tricks and techniques that would keep them alive.

In retrospect, his father had been like the senior member of his Delta Force team, weathered, knowledgeable and full of understanding only experience could give.

"I checked with the sheriff this morning," his mother said. "They don't have anything more on the attack last night. No others have reported anything similar, and they had a rather quiet night otherwise."

"I didn't figure they'd find anything, if we couldn't." Trace shook his head. "I'd like to get my hands on the bastard." He looked from his mother to Lily and back. "Take this threat seriously. No one is to go out after dark to take care of the animals without a backup. You must have a buddy."

"We're pretty shorthanded to have to wait for a buddy every time we need to run out to the barn," his mother said.

"I don't care," Trace said. "If it keeps you safe, that's all that matters."

His mother smiled. "That's what your father would have said."

Too many reminders of his father's absence made Trace wish he'd been home before his father died. Now he would never have the opportunity to fix the rift between them. His father wouldn't know that his son finally understood him.

Breakfast was finished in a few short minutes. Cleanup went just as quickly with all four of them helping to set the kitchen straight.

"Matt is meeting us at the attorney's office in thirty minutes." Trace's mother hung the damp dish towel to dry. "We need to get a move on."

"I'm driving," Trace said. "I need to pick up supplies on the way back. We'll go in my truck."

"That would be nice, since Lily was injured last

night." His mother slipped the strap of her purse over her arm and started for the door.

Lily opened her mouth and closed it again without arguing.

Trace was glad she hadn't insisted on driving. If they encountered any more threats, he wanted to be in control of the vehicle. He wasn't certain how the reading would go or how he would feel afterward. His mother was being far too secretive for his liking. Which probably meant he wasn't going to like what she and his father had decided would happen with the Whiskey Gulch Ranch. Though he'd told Irish he didn't care what his parents had decided, he cared about what happened to the family home and land. He didn't like the idea of it being split up and sold to the highest bidder.

"Be careful while we're gone," he said to Irish. "We'll get started harvesting hay as soon as we get back this afternoon."

Irish popped a salute. "I'll keep a close watch on the place and be ready to go when you return."

Dread sank like a lead weight to the pit of his belly. He knew he shouldn't let the contents of the will worry him so much, but it did.

Trace helped his mother into the passenger seat and closed the door.

Lily climbed into the back seat and buckled her seat belt.

By the time Trace slid into the driver's seat, the breakfast he'd consumed was roiling.

He had to tell himself that whatever happened, it was meant to be. He couldn't change it now. Frankly, he'd rather have his father back than have his father's ranch.

LILY SAT BEHIND Trace for the drive into town to the attorney's office. She made use of the time sitting in the back seat to study the man from behind.

Maybe it was an illusion, but he seemed taller than he had when he left to join the army. His shoulders were much broader and thickly muscled. His hair was cut in a crisp military style with the back and sides shaved short and the top a little longer, but not much. He carried himself straight and unbending, proud and sexy as hell. Her mouth tingled all over again at the memory of his lips on hers. Her body burned where his had touched hers the night before.

As she studied him, she caught Trace staring at her in the rearview mirror.

Heat rushed up her neck and suffused her cheeks. Leaning toward the side window, she moved out of range of his mirror and focused instead on the fields they passed on their way into town.

Why couldn't she focus on the coming meeting with Mr. Travis's attorney? Instead, she was mooning over a man she could never have. What would it get her? Absolutely nothing. The man was so far out of her league, he might as well be from another planet.

Sure, she was good enough to be a ranch hand or a housekeeper. But Trace deserved better than what she brought to the table. Besides, he'd never forgiven her for dumping him before he left for basic combat training. Telling him she'd been seeing Matt Hennessey had killed anything Trace might have had for her. As far as he was concerned, she'd been cheating on him. He'd cut her from his life and never once tried to contact her in the past eleven years.

She'd done it for him. If she'd stayed with him, he

might have given up on going into the army. He would have stayed with her and lived in the run-down trailer park where she lived just to spite his father. He'd have been miserable, and she would have felt guilty for not letting him go to join the army and get away from the ranch and his father.

No, she'd done the right thing for Trace. Losing him had broken her heart. She'd stayed in Whiskey Gulch, foolishly hoping that one day he would return and forgive her for the lie she'd told. After eleven years, she'd given up and resigned herself to life without Trace in it.

They pulled to a stop in front of the attorney's office beside an older truck with a smashed front fender.

"Roy's here." Rosalynn frowned. "I told him he didn't have to come. We could have called him with the outcome. Hopefully, he's up to this." She smiled and waved at the foreman.

Before anyone could get out of their vehicles, Matt rolled in beside them on his motorcycle.

Immediately, Trace tensed, and his hands tightened on the steering wheel until his knuckles turned white.

"Oh, good. Matt's here, too," his mother said.

Lily leaned to the right to catch a glimpse of Trace's face in the rearview mirror.

His lips had thinned, and his jaw was set in stone.

How truly unfortunate she had used Matt as the man she'd left Trace for.

Trace stepped out of the truck and helped his mother alight.

Roy exited his truck, sliding gingerly to the ground, wincing as his foot hit the pavement. "Mrs. Travis," he said with a nod. "You're looking good."

She nodded. "Thank you, Roy. I'm glad to see you're

getting around, though you should be at home with your foot up."

His lips slid into a smile. "Just like you to worry about everyone else. I'll be all right."

Rosalynn waved her hand toward the building. "Shall we?"

Matt reached the office door first and held it open. Mrs. Travis led the way inside, stopping at the reception desk. "Could you tell Mr. Phillips that Mrs. Travis and her party are here to see him?"

The woman behind the desk nodded and lifted her desk phone, announcing their guests. A moment later, she rose and led them into a conference room with a long table and a dozen chairs grouped around it.

"This really won't take long," Mrs. Travis said.

A man in a gray pin-striped suit entered the conference room with a folio tucked beneath his arm. He went straight to Mrs. Travis and hugged her. "I'm sorry you've had to come to me under these circumstances. You, James and I didn't expect we'd have to invoke the provisions of this will quite this soon."

She gave the attorney a watery smile. "Thankfully, we had the opportunity to put things in place before my husband passed. If you don't mind, we need to get right to it. We have hay to cut today."

"Perfect," Mr. Phillips said. He pulled out a chair, dropped his folio on the smooth dark wood of the conference table and took his seat.

With careful deliberation, Mr. Phillips opened the folio, extracted a document and laid it on the table. "I'm required to read this to you all. Please have a seat and bear with me."

Matt held Mrs. Travis's chair until she was seated and then took the chair beside her.

Trace sat on her other side, angry that Hennessey was even at the table.

Roy sat across the table from Trace.

Lily sat next to Roy with her hands in her lap.

"James and Rosalynn met with me a couple of months ago to iron out details and to record James's wishes in the following document." The attorney turned the cover over to the first page. "James was adamant the wording be such that anyone and everyone would understand what he wished to happen in the occurrence of his death."

Lily twisted her hands in her lap and wondered for the thousandth time why Mr. Travis had included her in the reading. They weren't related. She shared a glance across the table with Matt, also unrelated to the deceased. Why were they there with the family?

Her stomach twisted into a tight knot as her gaze shifted to Trace.

He turned to stare at his mother.

His mother met his gaze and held it while the attorney presented the will.

"Let me start by stating that, as his widow, Mrs. Travis is entitled to all of James Travis's estate. However, the couple wanted people close to them to receive certain holdings should one die before the other. They felt it important to make this happen sooner than later."

Mrs. Travis nodded silently.

The attorney drew in a deep breath and announced, "James Travis and Rosalynn Travis have set up a trust fund for Miss Lily Davidson to be paid out in monthly installments for the rest of her life."

Lily gasped. "What? I don't understand. I just work for the Travises. I'm not a blood relative." Her gaze shot to Trace.

He glanced at her briefly and then returned his gaze to his mother, his brow wrinkling slightly.

His mother nodded with a hint of a smile, as if saying it was okay.

"Mr. Travis wanted Lily to know he wasn't always fair when it came to his treatment of her." The attorney smiled toward Lily. "He wanted to make amends by ensuring you never had to worry about supporting yourself again."

Lily's eyes filled. "But I don't want his money. It belongs to his wife."

"What you do with it is now your business," the attorney said. "Let's continue."

Trace's mother reached out and covered Lily's hand with her own. "He wanted to do this. Please, let him."

The attorney went on. "To Roy Gibson, he left the ranch truck, knowing that if he passed and the ranch was sold, Roy would need a new truck to move on to his next place of employment if the new owners didn't employ him. If the ranch is sold, he's also to receive six months' pay, to tide him over until he can secure alternate employment."

Roy's eyes narrowed. "Mr. Travis didn't owe me anything. He gave me a job when I needed one."

"He knew how much you needed a better truck and wanted you to have the one you used on the ranch." Trace's mother smiled softly. "He cared about his employees."

"Those were the minor assignments," the attorney said. "The will leaves the rest of the estate to James

Travis's children to be held in a trust. If one chooses to sell his interest, the entire estate must be sold, the proceeds to be divided in equal shares."

Trace's brow dipped. "What do you mean, children?"

His mother leaned forward, her gaze pinning her son's. "Trace, your father and I wanted to tell you about this but didn't want to do it while you were deployed. It's something that needed to be done in person. You have a brother. Or rather, a half brother."

"What?" He shook his head, his gaze going from his mother to Lily and finally to Matt Hennessey, sitting at the same table with them. He looked as if he'd been punched in the gut. "You?"

Matt nodded slowly. "It was as much of a shock to me when I found out."

Trace turned back to his mother. "You've got to be kidding."

She shook her head. "No, sweetheart, I'm not. Your father didn't even know he had another child until Matt's mother was murdered, God rest her soul."

"How can a man not know he has another child?" His frown deepened. "Was he cheating on you?"

Mrs. Travis raised her hands. "No. No. It wasn't like that. Matt is two years older than you. James had been dating his mother when she got pregnant. Shortly after they stopped dating, she left Whiskey Gulch for a couple years. When she returned, she had a toddler with her. James never did the math. It wasn't until she passed a year ago that her lawyer sent a letter to James, informing him that he had a son by her. James felt awful that he hadn't known about Matt and that he'd missed knowing his son for all those years. This was his way of making it up to Matt."

Trace leaned back in his seat, shaking his head. "By giving him the ranch?"

"By giving you *both* the ranch. He wanted to leave it to his sons." She looked from Trace to Matt and back to Trace again. "But he didn't want it split up."

"Then why the hell did he leave it to the two of us?" Trace pushed back from the table. "How do you even know he's really my father's son?"

"Matt was as concerned about it as you." Mrs. Travis nodded toward Matt. "When he learned the truth, he offered to have a DNA test conducted. The results were 99.9 percent conclusive. He's your father's son."

Lily sat in stunned silence, trying to take it all in.

Not only had Trace's father left her money, which would only make Trace madder that his inheritance was going to the woman who'd cheated on him, but now he was locked into dual ownership of the Whiskey Gulch Ranch with a man he barely knew. A man who, it turns out, was his brother.

If she thought there was even the slightest chance at a reconciliation between the two of them, there was no way it would happen now.

Chapter Eight

Trace leaned back in his chair, his head spinning, anger burning in his belly. At that moment, he wished he was back in Afghanistan fighting bad guys. That was easier than dealing with his father's last wishes. Even from his grave, his father was dictating his life for him.

"There's more legalese in the document, but that's what it all boils down to," the attorney said. "I suggest you take time to think about it. If either of you decide to sell your portion, the entire ranch will have to be sold. Your mother would have to give up her home and find another place to live. It was James's hope that his two sons would come to an agreement on how to manage the ranch holdings and keep it in the family for another one hundred years. He also understood these are changing times and owning land might not be as appealing to the younger generation. He didn't want the ranch to be a burden. Mrs. Travis will retain a portion of the assets to see her through the end of her life. James left her a small cottage in town she can choose to move into or sell."

"Mom." Trace stared at his mother. "You let him do this?"

She nodded. "I knew I wouldn't want to run the

ranch without your father. He was what made it so successful. Not me. It was his to give. Not mine. I didn't
mind taking care of it until you two came on board, but
I'm not the one to do this. I want to cook, crochet and
help raise grandbabies." She gave him a gentle smile.
"And if you decide to sell, I don't need the money. I
have plenty of my own. I can start over wherever I decide to go."

"It's your home," Trace said. "You should be able to
live there the rest of your life."

"Without your father, it's not the same." She
shrugged. "I knew that's how it would be. I told him I
didn't want the ranch if he passed before me. It belongs
to his children and their children's children…if that's
the route you two choose to go."

Her comment brought him back to the table and the
man seated so near. Trace jerked a thumb toward him.
"He's never worked a day on the ranch. Why leave it
to him?"

"Your father regrets that he didn't get to know Matt
while he was growing up. He couldn't undo the past,
but he was determined to make it right for the future.
Both you and Matt are his children. By leaving the
ranch in a trust for both of you, he'd hoped to bring
you together as brothers."

"He could never be a brother to me," Trace said.
"My brothers are Irish, Levi and Beck—men from my
team. They've had my back since I joined the force."

"Goes both ways. The only brothers I've known are
the ones I met in the Marine Corps," Matt said. "And
like Trace said, I know nothing about ranching." He
glanced at Trace's mother. "I'm sorry. I offered to help
you, and I will. But long-term…it just won't work."

"And I'm scheduled to go back on active duty when things settle down here," Trace said.

For a brief second, his mother winced, then a mask settled over her expression. "This has all been a shock to you two. All I ask is that you think about it for a few days. Even if you end up selling the ranch, you need to keep it running, take care of the animals and prepare for winter by stockpiling hay. And that doesn't even take into account the threat that's hanging over everything. Someone is causing problems that could impact the sale of the land and cattle."

Trace clenched his teeth. He didn't want to have to work with Hennessey, but they had to do something to bring closure to the danger. "You're right, we have to neutralize the threat. Until then, no one is safe on the ranch. I'll table the discussion until I've had more time to resolve issues and come to a decision."

Hennessey nodded. "Agreed. And I'll still help haul hay. I might not know much about ranching, but I'm not afraid of hard work."

Trace's mother smiled at Matt and then at Trace. "A little time and help is all I ask. Thank you."

The attorney gave them copies of the will and his condolences and escorted them out of the building.

Matt mounted his motorcycle and pulled on his helmet. "I'll see you at the ranch." He started his engine and roared away.

Roy limped out behind them, took Trace's mother's hands and squeezed them. "I'm really sorry about your loss. Mr. Travis was a decent man and a good boss."

"Thank you, Roy," she said, ducking her head. "He was a good man."

"I'll be back at the ranch soon. I think I can get back to work at least at some of the light duty."

"Take your time," Rosalynn said. "Now that Trace is home, Lily and I have help."

Roy nodded. "Nevertheless, I need to get back to work. I don't like the idea of you being out there on your own, in case someone turns on you." He gave her an awkward hug and stepped back.

She smiled. "I'm okay for now." She turned her smile toward Trace. "I have my son to protect me."

Roy slid into his truck, rolled down the window and tipped his head, first toward Trace and then Rosalynn. "Take good care of her. Your mother is special."

"I know."

Trace helped his mother into the truck while Lily slipped quietly into the back seat. When he started to turn left and head toward the ranch, his mother reminded him, "Don't we need some supplies at the feed store?"

He altered his direction and drove to the store, his thoughts still on what the attorney had said and the fact his mother had known about Matt being his half brother but hadn't told him.

At the feed store, Lily and his mother got out along with him and went inside.

Forcing himself to focus on what he needed, he mentally checked off his list one item at a time.

"Mrs. Travis, sorry to hear about your husband," a voice said one aisle over from him.

"Good morning, Chad," his mother said. "Thank you for your concern."

Trace grabbed a new brush and curry comb from the

shelf and walked to the end of the aisle to see the face of the man who was talking to her.

He was a tall, lean man, wearing jeans, a denim shirt and worn cowboy boots. It had been years since Trace had seen him, but he recognized the man as Chad Meyers, the owner of the Rafter M Ranch adjacent to the Whiskey Gulch Ranch.

"How's Alice?" his mother asked.

"She's doing better since she had that back operation. Not getting around as fast as she'd hoped, but better."

"Tell her I'm thinking of her." His mother smiled up at Mr. Meyers. "I'll try to get by this week to check on her."

"We were shocked to hear about what happened to James." The man shook his head. "We had our differences, but I didn't wish ill will on the man."

His mother patted Mr. Meyers's arm. "I'm sure you both meant well. Tell Alice hello for me."

Mr. Meyers thanked her and moved away.

"You all right?" Trace asked.

His mother gave him a tight smile, her eyes glassy with unshed tears. "It'll take time." She left him and walked over to say hello to another neighbor.

"Talk about disagreements, Meyers and your father had a bit of an argument right here in the feed store last week," a voice said behind him.

Trace turned to face a man with white-blond hair and gray eyes. "Do I know you?"

The man held out his hand. "Oswald Young. I own the property north of the Whiskey Gulch Ranch."

Trace frowned as he shook the man's hand. The only ranch he knew of to the north was the Rocking J, owned by the Johnsons. "Which property?"

"The Rocking J," Oswald said. "Purchased most of it from Ken and Minnie Johnson six months ago. They couldn't keep up with it anymore and they didn't have family to leave it to."

"I didn't know that." He'd known the Johnsons all his life. "I went to school with their son."

"Apparently, he didn't want the ranch. They were ready to sell and…right place, right time. Now I'm the owner of thirty-two hundred acres of the Rocking J Ranch."

"Congratulations," Trace said, though he couldn't care less about the man's purchase.

"We're setting up an outfitting service for game hunters. The land is full of wild hogs, turkey, white-tailed and axis deer. We hope to introduce buffalo and elk as well." The man puffed out his chest and grinned broadly. "We have big plans."

"Interesting," Trace said, searching for his mother… or anyone who could extricate him from his new neighbor's conversation.

Lily appeared at Trace's side. "Your mother is ready to go."

"Nice to meet you, neighbor," Oswald said. "See ya around."

Trace carried his items to the counter, ordered several bags of feed and paid. His mother stood beside him, greeting townspeople who stepped up to pay their respects and condolences for her loss.

Oswald approached her, his smile gone, his brow furrowed. "Mrs. Travis, I'm so sorry for your loss. Please accept my sincere condolences. If there's anything we can do at the Rocking J, just let us know." He reached for her hand and held it in both of his.

"Thank you, Mr. Young."

"Please, call me Oswald."

"Oswald," Trace's mother said.

"And, Mrs. Travis… If for any reason you decide to sell the Whiskey Gulch Ranch, please, let me know. We're looking to expand the Rocking J even more."

Trace's mother winced.

If Trace hadn't been watching her, he wouldn't have seen her pain. He wanted to punch Oswald Young square in the face but knew it would only upset his mother further. Instead, he stepped between his mother and Mr. Young. "Let's go, Mom." He hooked his mother's elbow in his grip and led her toward the door. By the time they left the store, his mother's face was pale, and she looked more fragile than Trace had ever seen her.

He helped her into the truck and closed the door.

Lily stood beside him. "It's been too much. She's been holding up for too long, bottling it in. I don't know how she hasn't broken down."

"We need to get her home." Trace thought about the word *home*. His mother and father had just given their home to him and a stranger. The shock had yet to wear off. Why would his mother do that? The ranch was just as much hers as it was his father's. She'd put every bit of her love and hard work into making it a profitable business and home for her family. He couldn't let her just move out and take up residence in a cottage in town, or God forbid, Florida.

Anger burned in Trace's gut. Even from his grave, his father was still calling the shots.

Trace couldn't wrap his mind around what was happening or what the future might hold, but he had to keep his mother safe and help her find happiness after the death of the only man she'd ever loved.

He climbed into the truck and turned to his mother. "Think you can stand to be in town for a little longer? I want to stop by the sheriff's office for a minute."

She nodded. "I'm all right. I'm more concerned about you."

Trace shook his head. "Don't be. You worry about you."

Her smile was crooked, but gentle. "I'm your mother. No matter how old you get, I'll always worry about you."

Trace drove to the sheriff's office. "Do you want to come in with me?" he asked.

His mother shook her head. "I'll wait here."

He didn't like leaving her in the truck but understood her reluctance to meet with the sheriff and dredge up all the pain of what had happened to his father. "I won't be long."

LILY OPENED THE back door of the pickup. "I'm coming." She slipped out of the truck and paused. Then she opened the passenger seat door and looked up at the woman who'd taken her in and treated her like family. "Will you be all right on your own?"

Rosalynn nodded. "I'm fine, just a little tired."

Lily lifted Trace's mother's hand and pressed it to her cheek. "Hang in there. You're surrounded by the people who love you."

Rosalynn curled her fingers around Lily's cheek. "I know. Now go. See if the sheriff has learned anything new. You can tell me all about it on the way home."

Lily closed the door and met Trace on the sidewalk

in front of the truck. He opened the sheriff's office door for her and held it as she entered.

Her heartbeat fluttered as she brushed past him. She could smell the outdoorsy scent that was solely Trace, and her knees wobbled just a little.

Inside, the sheriff stood at the counter, talking to one of his deputies. When he spotted Lily and Trace, he turned and held out his hand to Lily first. "Lily, I'm glad you came."

"Sheriff Owens, you remember Trace Travis?" Lily said.

The sheriff nodded and offered his hand to Trace. "I do. I was still just a deputy the day he hopped on the bus to join the army. I remember his mother seeing him off." He shook Trace's hand. "Good to see you back. I'm sorry for the circumstances."

Trace dipped his head. "Good to see you, Sheriff Owens. Congratulations on moving up in the department."

"Don't know what possessed me to run for sheriff, but the town voted me in. Guess I better do right by them." He winked. "What can I do for you?"

"What's happening with the investigation on my father's murder?" Trace asked.

The sheriff waved them toward a hallway. "Come to the conference room. We have the investigation laid out in there."

Lily followed the sheriff into the conference room, fully aware of Trace right behind her. Her body was tuned into his nearness, her nerves hopping at every chance brush of his skin against hers.

The room had a long table in the middle with chairs all around and a long whiteboard stretched across one entire wall. Names were written in black. Lily recognized many of the names, including some of the people who'd worked on Whiskey Gulch Ranch—Roy Gibson, their foreman, and Marty Bains and Alan Holden, the ranch hands who'd bailed as soon as things got hot on the ranch. Beside their names were those of the neighbors whose land bordered the Travises' ranch—Oswald Young of the Rocking J, Chad and Alice Meyers of the Rafter M Ranch. Matt Hennessey's name was listed alongside Lily's and some random townsfolk. There were other names Lily didn't recognize. The name on the board that surprised her most was Rosalynn Travis.

Lily frowned. "Are all of these people suspects in Mr. Travis's murder?"

The sheriff shook his head. "Not necessarily. We list all those close to the victim in proximity, people who owed James money and family ties who were present when the murder occurred." He nodded toward Trace. "You're not on the board because you were deployed at the time."

Trace's eyes narrowed. "You don't think my mother or Lily killed my father, do you?"

"No, we don't," Sheriff Owens said. "But we have to talk to everyone who might have seen something or might know of someone with a motive to kill your father." He pointed to the board. "We've questioned every one of the people listed on the board so far."

"And?"

The sheriff shook his head. "So far, we haven't identified anyone with a motive." He pointed to Marty and Alan's names. "The ranch hands weren't even close to Mr. Travis when he was shot. They had just left for town with Miss Lily to get more supplies for the barnyard gate they'd been working on when Mr. Travis's horse brought him home."

"Roy had gone to town that morning," Lily murmured, remembering that horrible day. The images flashing through her mind made her stomach roil.

The sheriff nodded. "That's the day he crashed his truck into a tree and hurt his foot. He hobbled the rest of the way into town after the wreck."

"What about the neighbors?" Trace asked. "We've known the Meyerses all my life. I can't imagine they'd have a motive for killing my father."

"They are in dire financial straits," the sheriff said. "But Mr. Meyers claims he was home with his wife all day. She's recovering from back surgery and requires someone to be with her at all times."

"The new owners of the Rocking J?" Lily asked. "Mr. Young asked Rosalynn if she wanted to sell the ranch."

The sheriff nodded. "We did ask him where he was at the time of the murder. He was with a group of hunters at the new lodge he had built on the property. They can all vouch for his and everyone else's whereabouts."

"Which leaves us back at ground zero," Trace said.

"It would help if we could find where he was actually shot. He could have been anywhere on his spread. We sent out twenty deputies and volunteers to look. With over twelve hundred acres to search, we didn't know where to begin. We did our best, but it wasn't good enough. Finding a bullet casing or tracks was nearly impossible. And the ground was hard and dry, not conducive to making tracks if someone had been on foot, on horseback or in a vehicle." The sheriff sighed. "I'm sorry I can't tell you more. We're running background checks on Oswald, since he's new in town. Other than that, all we can think is some random poacher might not have been watching where he was shooting and hit your father by accident. It's been known to happen."

Trace nodded. "Thanks for trying." He shook the sheriff's hand. "You'll keep us informed if you hear anything else?"

"You bet," said Sheriff Owens.

Trace led Lily out of the office. "I'd like to talk to the ranch hands sometime soon."

"They had been working on a gate in the barnyard. They didn't do it. I was there all day."

"Yeah, but they might know something about what was going on around the place."

Lily's lips firmed. "They're just a bunch of cowards, more interested in where they could get their next beer."

"Agreed. Any man who'd leave two women unprotected after something like that isn't worthy of working on this ranch," Trace murmured. He opened the back door of the pickup and waited for Lily to climb in. Once she was settled, he stared up at her. "Thank you for being here for Mom," he whispered.

"I heard that," his mother said from the front passenger seat. "She's been a blessing. I couldn't have done it without her."

Lily's cheeks heated. "I did only what a decent person would have done." She nodded at Trace. "I love your mother. I'd do it all again."

Trace's gaze met hers for a moment longer, sending a ripple of a different kind of heat through her body.

Then he shut the door and slid in behind the steering wheel. The moment was gone, but the feeling lingered all the way back to the ranch.

Irish and Matt were waiting in the barnyard when Trace parked the truck.

Lily braced for his anger at seeing Matt again.

Trace didn't say a word. He might not like the result of the will, but he couldn't turn away help when they had so much work to do.

Lily hooked Rosalynn's arm and escorted her into the house. She made her a cup of iced tea and had her sit in the air-conditioned living room. "With Trace, Matt and Irish out there cutting hay, they won't need me. I'll take care of the animals and dinner. You rest. It's been a hard day. You stay here, I'll get some things together for the guys."

Lily hurried to the kitchen, filled an insulated jug full of ice and water, and made six sandwiches out of the leftover ham a neighbor had brought over the night before. After she wrapped the sandwiches and stored them in a sturdy basket, she carried them out to the barn, where the men were unloading the supplies from Trace's pickup.

Lily handed the jug and the basket to Irish. "You'll need this out there."

He smiled and thanked her.

Before Trace and Matt emerged from the barn, she was back at the house, glad to have avoided the awkwardness of being in the presence of the two men together. At one point in the near future, she would own up to the fact she'd lied about being in love with Matt. At the very least, it might ease the tension between the brothers.

Lily returned to the living room to find Rosalynn where she'd left her.

The older woman smiled. "Thank you, Lily. I don't

know what I would have done without you the past few days."

She hugged Rosalynn. "I'm glad I was here to help. You've done so much for me."

The older woman shook her head. "Sweetie, you've done more for me and James."

"You two gave me a job and a place to live. That's pretty big." Lily stared down at the woman who'd come to mean so much to her. "I don't know why you and James did what you did."

"James wanted to gift you with security. He felt so badly about how he treated you when you were dating Trace. He didn't know you and judged you unfairly."

Lily shrugged. "He didn't have to do what he did to make up for it. We'd come to a pretty good understanding of each other over the past year. I loved him like the father I wished I'd had growing up."

Rosalynn took her hand. "He felt like you were the daughter he never had. He only wished he'd figured that out sooner." She squeezed Lily's fingers. "Let us do this for you."

Lily frowned. "It's too much. I don't need that kind of money."

"He wasn't sure how things would turn out on the ranch if he passed and the boys inherited." Trace's mother looked toward the window that overlooked the barn and the men gathering around a tractor.

"Do you think they'll work it out?" Lily stared out at the same view, her gaze seeking Trace.

"I don't know," Rosalynn said. "Trace loves being a part of the Delta Force. He'd have to give it up to come home. I'm not sure ranching life would be enough to keep him happy."

"He always loved the animals and the wide-open spaces," Lily offered, knowing Trace's mother was right. The man had been fighting wars. Ranching would mean slowing down. On the selfish side, she'd love if he was back for good, even if he wasn't back for her.

"I only need a few minutes of rest," Rosalynn said. "No need for you to handle everything by yourself. I'll help with dinner and with feeding the animals. I don't want you out there on your own while the men are away in the field."

"I'll be all right. Now that I know there might be someone lurking in the shadows of the barn, I'll be hyperaware and keep my eyes open for danger."

The older woman shook her head. "I can't risk it. You know Trace will insist on the buddy system."

Lily settled in the seat beside Rosalynn's. "Then I'll wait with you until you're ready to go out. We've had an eventful morning and could use the rest." No sooner had she settled on the seat, she popped up. "Let me get us both a fresh glass of iced tea." She gathered Rosalynn's glass, hurried to the kitchen to refill it and poured one for herself. Lily laid the glasses on a tray, added a small plate full of cookies from the cookie jar and returned to the living room.

"Thank you, Lily." Rosalynn took the glass of tea and a cookie and waited for Lily to settle beside her.

"You've been working here for over a year, but you never talked about what happened between you and Trace." Rosalynn took a bite of the cookie and pinned Lily with a curious stare.

Lily took a sip of her tea and swallowed hard before she met Trace's mother's gaze. "It didn't work out."

"Was it because of the big argument he had with

his father? You knew about it, didn't you?" Rosalynn sighed. "James wanted the best for his son."

"And I wasn't the best," Lily added.

"It wasn't until you came to work for us that James got to know you. He regretted what he'd said to our son. On more than one occasion, he told me he wished Trace had married you. You would have been good for him."

"Your husband was right. Trace was going into the military. If I'd stayed with him, his association with me and my family could have hindered him getting the security clearance he needed."

"So you let him go without you," Rosalynn said.

Lily bent her head for a moment and then looked up again, her chest tight. "I told him I was in love with someone else. When he asked who, the only person I could think of was the guy with the worst reputation in the community at that time."

"Oh, dear Lord." Rosalynn's eyes widened. "Was that someone else Matt Hennessey?"

Lily nodded.

"Matt Hennessey, the man who stole you from him and now has stolen half his legacy." Rosalynn smacked her hand to her forehead. "No wonder he was so angry at the law office."

"Trace never forgave me for telling him that I was in love with another man," Lily said. "I can't blame him. I'm sure my announcement came to him out of left field. I had to do something to make sure he left and there wasn't a reason for the people who performed the background checks to come looking for me or my family. He didn't need to have any strikes against him when he entered the military. I'm not certain how closely they would have checked into his friends and acquaintances, but having a girlfriend from my background wouldn't have helped him in the least."

"You're not responsible for your family's actions."

"I know that, but no one else seems to take that into account." Lily shrugged. "Guilt by association. I don't have to tell you. Everyone in the county knows that my father is in jail. My mother has a questionable occupation and has been in and out of jail herself."

"You're a good person, Lily. Anyone who gets close to you knows that," Rosalynn said. "Trace knows that, deep down. He'll figure it out."

Lily shook her head. "It's okay. After eleven years, I've gotten over him. We were young and stupid. Trace has his life now and I have mine."

"But you two were meant for each other," Trace's mother said.

"Don't," Lily said. "We're over each other. That was a long time ago. We have more important things to worry about right now. I'd appreciate if you didn't talk with Trace about our past. We're on different paths now."

"You're living under the same roof," Rosalynn pointed out.

Lily gave her a tight smile. "That's just logistics, not love."

"Oh, but life is too short," Rosalynn said, her eyes filling with tears. "You have to grab for the joy and hold on to it for as long as you can."

"I'll keep that in mind. In the meantime, I'm going to see what we can thaw out for dinner." Lily hurried out of the living room before Rosalynn noticed the tears in her own eyes. There had been a time when she'd been filled with the joy of love and laughter. When she and Trace had been young and head over heels in love.

Eleven years was long enough to forget how good they'd had it, wasn't it?

Chapter Nine

When Trace drove the first tractor out of the shed he noticed a wet black spot in the dirt where the vehicle had been parked.

"Something's leaking," he said as he dropped down from the enclosed cab.

"I'm pretty good with engines," Matt said. "Let me take a look."

Trace stiffened. He'd worked on tractor engines from the time he was tall enough to reach the hood. Granted, the tractor he was looking at was a newer model than what he'd worked on in his youth, and it had been eleven years since he'd tinkered with engines. But he just wasn't ready to let Matt into his world. If he ever would be ready. "I'll check it."

After a few minutes and banging his knuckles a couple times, he realized it would take him a lot longer to figure out the engine and all its components. Because he didn't have time to call in a mechanic, and they really needed to get that hay cut, Trace knew he had to step aside and let Matt take over. It grated on his nerves and he ground his teeth. Short of waiting a day or two for a mechanic, he had to let go of this one thing.

He straightened and turned to Matt, who leaned

against the barn, his arms crossed over his chest, his eyebrow cocked.

"I don't have time for this. If you think you can fix it, have at it." He stepped aside.

Matt didn't move from his relaxed position. "Say please."

It took every bit of his limited restraint to keep from punching the bastard in his smug face. "Please," Trace gritted out.

With the hint of a cocky grin, Matt pushed away from the side of the barn. Within minutes, he had parts pulled loose or pushed aside.

Trace hoped the man wasn't making it worse.

"Give me a radio, computer or weapons, and I can disassemble and reassemble in a heartbeat," Irish said. "Vehicle engines? Not so much. I left those to the mechanics in the motor pool."

Matt worked silently, retrieved a small tool kit from the storage compartment on his bike, twisted something, tapped something and reassembled the parts. After returning his tools to his bike, he faced Irish and Trace. "Should be good to go."

Trace climbed aboard the tractor and fired up the engine. One explosive backfire and the engine hummed to life. He pulled forward a few feet, stopped, set the brake and climbed down. Nothing dripped to the earth below.

He didn't want to feel anything toward the half brother who'd stolen his girl and half his legacy. But Trace's sense of fairness overruled his desire to strike out at the man. "Thanks."

"I'll get the other tractor out while you attach whatever implement you need," Matt said.

Trace's inclination was to tell Matt he didn't need

the help, but he did, and refusing it would only be petty and childish. Instead, he nodded.

"The sooner we get the hay cut, the sooner it will dry and we can bale." He attached the mower to the three-point hitch of the first tractor.

Matt entered the shed and a few minutes later had the second, smaller tractor out. This one didn't have the air-conditioned cab like the first. He checked the oil, hoses and tires. Trace helped Matt attach another mower to the second tractor. After they filled the tanks, they parked the tractors near the gate to the field that needed to be cut.

Trace returned to Irish, who waited in front of the barn. "Got another tractor?" he asked.

"No. I have a more important job for you while we're mowing." Trace entered the shed one more time. His father kept two four-wheelers inside. He found only one. Had his father gotten rid of the other? As soon as the thought surfaced, Trace shook his head. The man never threw away anything. He'd keep it for spare parts before he let it go. He'd ask Roy about it when the man came back to work. In the meantime, he started the re-maining four-wheeler and drove it out of the shed. "Get your rifle," Trace said to Irish. "We need you to cover us while we're mowing."

Irish grinned. "Finally, something I can do until my stitches heal." He hurried back to his vehicle and laid out a case. Inside the case was an AR-15, much like the M4 Carbine rifle they'd used in Afghanistan. He loaded it with a thirty-round magazine of bullets and shoved a couple more magazines into the pockets of a vest. He strapped on a shoulder holster, tucked a Glock into the holster and slipped the vest over it. When he turned, he grinned. "Ready."

"I've never been that ammoed up to ride out on the ranch," Trace said, his gut twisting.

Irish frowned. "Too much?"

Trace raised his hand with a grin. "No way. I'm not complaining. I guess it's a sign of the times."

"I don't know what's been going on around here, but I learned in the deserts of Iraq and the mountains of Afghanistan you can never carry too much ammo." Irish climbed aboard the ATV, revved the engine and followed the two men through the gate, closing it behind them.

The field to be mowed was thirty acres of tall grass the cattle and horses had not been allowed to graze.

Trace and Matt started at the same end of the field, Trace making the first row and Matt holding back long enough to start the second row. They worked closely together that afternoon to make it easier to provide protection for both of them.

Irish rode the four-wheeler around the perimeter of the field and then set up a position where he could keep an eye on both men driving the tractors, while watching the wooded area bordering the southern end of the field.

Mowing was hot and dusty. Trace tied a bandanna over his mouth and nose and forged ahead. Even inside the cab of the larger tractor, he was inundated with fine particles of dirt. The time Trace spent on the tractor gave him plenty of opportunity to ruminate on what the attorney and his mother had said about Matt being his half brother and the stipulations of their combined inheritance. The angry man inside of him made him want to sell the ranch to keep Matt from getting any portion of the Travis lands. Hadn't the man taken enough from him?

First he'd taken Lily, now his family's legacy.

But was it Matt's fault their father felt so guilty that he wanted to make amends for never having spent time with his first son? Hell, James Travis could have decided to leave it all to Matt. Even if he didn't raise him, he was his firstborn.

Dust rose as they cut the hay, making the Texas sunshine hazy and hard to see through. When they'd made it halfway through the mowing, Trace parked his tractor at one end of the field and waited for Matt to catch up.

After turning off his tractor, Matt asked, "Is there a problem?"

"Thought we'd let the engines cool while we get a drink and have lunch."

"I don't need a break, if you want to push through and get it done," Matt said.

"We're making good progress," Trace said. "It won't hurt to break for fifteen minutes and give the tractors time to cool off and us a chance to recharge."

Matt dropped down off his machine and stretched.

Irish rode up on the four-wheeler. "Is it lunchtime?"

Trace frowned. "Takes too much time to go back to the house. I thought we'd just take a break and get back to it."

"We don't have to go back to the house." Irish grinned. "I have lunch in the storage container."

"When did you get that?" Trace asked.

"Lily handed me a basket before we left. I'm not sure what she packed in here." He opened the plastic container and extracted the basket. One at a time, he pulled out neatly wrapped sandwiches.

Trace's heart swelled. Even when she wasn't with them, she was thinking of the men working on the ranch.

Matt bit into one of the sandwiches, chewed and swallowed. "I need to marry that girl. She's a keeper."

Trace's hand froze halfway to his mouth. His blood boiled. He tried but failed to keep his anger under control. "Are you kidding me? You had your chance and blew it."

Matt jerked back as if Trace had hit him. "What the heck are you talking about?"

"You know damn well what I'm talking about." Trace advanced on Matt. "You were supposed to marry Lily, and you dumped her."

"Back off, Travis. You don't know what you're talking about." Matt's eyes narrowed. "You're just mad because *our* father didn't leave you his entire estate."

"I couldn't care less if my father gave you all of this ranch. You still did Lily wrong, and I won't let you break her heart a second time."

"I don't know why you think I broke her heart. I don't love Lily like that."

"Well, she sure as hell was in love with you."

"You're insane," Matt said.

"Uh, Trace," Irish interrupted, "this argument isn't getting the work done."

Trace ignored his friend and stood toe to toe with Matt Hennessey. "You're my father's bastard son bent on stealing from me and my family." Trace punched Matt in the gut.

Matt swung for Trace's face, his knuckles connecting with Trace's jaw.

Trace staggered backward, regained his balance and charged toward Matt.

The crack of gunfire split the air and a puff of dust exploded at Trace's feet. Immediately, Trace, Matt and Irish dropped to the ground.

Irish came up in a prone shooting position and aimed into the woods.

Trace rolled beneath the tractor, pulled his Glock from the holster on his hip and studied the woods.

An engine rumbled somewhere in the trees and underbrush. An ATV took off through the shadows, headed away from where the men lay in the dirt.

Trace leaped to his feet and ran for the four-wheeler, hopped aboard and raced after the departing rider. He lurched across the field and into the woods, dodging trees and underbrush.

For a moment, he thought he'd lost the ATV in front of him. Then a flash in the shadows caught his attention. He yanked the handlebars to the left and hit the accelerator, careening through the woods. In an effort to cut off the guy in front of him, he swerved to the right, then dived into a ditch and back up the other side, veering in front of the other ATV.

The driver jerked his handlebars to the right, on a collision course to slam into Trace.

With little time to react, Trace pulled hard to the right, narrowly missed a tree, dipped down into a ditch and slammed the four-wheeler into a fallen log.

When the ATV stopped so suddenly, Trace flew over the handlebars, flipped in midair and landed hard on his back. With the wind knocked from his lungs, he lay still, unable to move for the next several seconds.

The roar of the ATV engine waned and then roared as the rider circled around and came full tilt at Trace.

Trace was just getting to his knees when the ATV stopped just short of him. The driver leveled a sawed-off shotgun, aiming at Trace's chest.

A shot rang out.

Too late to move, Trace held his breath and braced for the hit and the pain.

When nothing happened, he looked down at his chest, fully expecting to see blood.

Nothing.

He dropped low to the ground, his gaze shifting back to the shooter.

The man on the ATV jerked backward, dropping the sawed-off shotgun across his legs. Clutching his shoulder with one hand, he turned the ATV and drove into the woods, disappearing into the shadows.

"What the—" Trace spun and looked back the way he'd come.

A silhouette of a man stood in the woods, a rifle pressed to his shoulder. When the man lowered it, Trace could see that it was Matt.

The man who'd stolen his girl and half of his inheritance had just saved his life.

LATE THAT AFTERNOON, Lily stood on the back porch, shading her eyes as she peered into the setting sun.

The men had yet to return from the hayfield, which shouldn't have taken them all afternoon to cut. What was keeping them?

"Think one of the tractors broke down?" Rosalynn asked from behind her.

"I don't know," Lily said. Her heart squeezed hard

in her chest. She didn't want to say it, but she was afraid for the men. Someone had it out for the people of Whiskey Gulch Ranch. "If they don't come home in the next five minutes, we'll take the truck and go check on them."

Rosalynn stepped up beside Lily and raised her hand to shade her eyes as she stared out across the pasture. "I'm ready whenever you are. I've already lost one member of my family. I don't want to lose another."

"You're not going to." Lily patted Mrs. Travis's arm. "Trace has all that combat training. He knows how to take care of himself and others. He's fine."

"I hope so."

"He is."

A tractor appeared on the horizon, a dark shape growing larger as it moved closer, stirring up dust as it rolled across the land. That was one.

Lily held her breath until the other tractor appeared behind it. "There they are."

"Good," Rosalynn said. "I'll put the dinner rolls in the oven." The older woman turned and entered the house.

Lily remained on the porch until the tractors got closer. Then she hurried out to the gate.

As they neared, she noticed the tractor in the rear of the procession had the four-wheeler following too close to be safe. Only it didn't have a rider.

Lily frowned and shaded her eyes. Someone stood behind the driver of the second tractor, holding onto the back of his seat. The second tractor didn't have the mower behind it. Instead, a heavy-duty strap was attached to the rear of the farm machinery and the front of the mangled four-wheeler.

Matt drove the first tractor through the gate. Trace, with Irish perched behind him, entered with the other.

Her gaze on the second driver, Lily's eyes widened, and her pulse raced.

Trace's face had a gash and a bruise on one cheekbone and his shirt appeared to be torn and dirty. Nothing like what she would have expected for a day seated on a tractor.

As soon as they stopped the tractors, she converged on him. "What happened to you?"

Trace shot a glance toward Matt. "I fell."

Matt rubbed his belly. "The hell he did. He got the bruise on his face when he punched me in the gut. He might not have realized I punch back."

With a shrug, Trace nodded. "He got that right. I did punch him first and fully deserved the punch he returned."

"Damn right he did." Matt stepped down from his tractor.

Lily frowned. "Did he knock you down and roll you around in the dirt as well?"

Matt snorted.

Trace waited for Irish to dismount from behind his seat before he stood and brushed some of the dust from his shirt.

"No," Trace said. "The rest was from when I fell off the ATV."

"You fell off the ATV?" Lily glanced at the four-wheeler they had towed behind the tractor. The front rack was bent, the handlebar was crooked, and there was dirt and leaves jammed in places that shouldn't have dirt and leaves. "What happened?"

Trace climbed down and stretched, wincing. "I hit a fallen log."

Irish stepped around him and unhooked the strap they'd used to haul the four-wheeler back to the barn. "He hit the fallen log after he was nearly run over."

"Run over?" Lily shook her head. "By one of the tractors?"

"No," Matt said. "By the shooter."

Lily's heartbeat stuttered. "Wait. What shooter?" She turned to Trace. "Someone shot at you?"

"Yeah. And I went after him." He glanced toward the house. "It's not a big deal. I wouldn't mention it in front of my mother. The shooter must have been a really bad shot."

"No big deal?" Lily threw her hands in the air. "Are you kidding me?"

His lips quirked. "Are you worried someone shot at me, or that you can't tell my mother?"

"This isn't some kind of joke. Your father was killed by a shooter. You've been shot at. Someone hit me in the barn. The Whiskey Gulch Ranch is under attack and you're afraid to tell your mother?" Her pulse still hammering through her veins, Lily marched toward the house. "I'm calling the sheriff. You can go back out and play Russian roulette with your shooter. I'm going to make sure your mother is taken care of when they drag your body back to the house."

Lily's chest hurt. Trace could have been shot and killed today. Her eyes stung and she wanted to vomit. How could he be so flippant?

A hand caught her arm and spun her around. "I'm sorry. I didn't know you cared so much."

She stared at the hand on her arm, wanting to fling

herself into his embrace. She clenched her fists and held on to her control by a thread. He could have been killed. For a long moment, she fought the urge to throw herself into his arms, pound his chest, then kiss him until he loved her, too.

Instead, she drew herself up and lifted her chin. "I'm calling the sheriff. This cannot continue. Your mother would be devastated if she lost you, too."

He didn't let go of her arm. "And you? Would you be devastated?"

She stared into his eyes, wanting to tell him just how broken her heart would be. "I'd hate to see your mother go through that kind of loss again." Then she shook her arm free of his grip and ran for the house.

She didn't look back but burst through the door into the house and let the screen slam shut behind her.

Rosalynn hurried out of the kitchen, carrying a wooden spoon. "What's wrong?"

"Ask your son," she said and went straight to the phone in the hallway. "I have a phone call to make." She dialed 911. When the dispatcher answered, Lily said, "I'd like to report a shooting."

Rosalynn gasped behind her and ran out the back door.

After she finished her call to the sheriff's office, Lily felt a twinge of guilt. Mrs. Travis didn't need the stress of hearing about a shooting after losing her husband the same way. But, damn it, Trace couldn't die. It would kill his mother.

Lily clasped her hands together and pressed them to her chest. "And it would kill me, too."

Chapter Ten

"Wade Richard Travis, you are not going back out in that hayfield. Not if I have anything to say about it." Rosalynn Travis stood with her hands fisted on her hips, a frown denting her brow.

Trace wanted to shake Lily for telling his mother about the shooting. But Lily was right to report it to the sheriff. At the very least, they could be asking around and on the lookout for anyone who showed up at any of the nearby clinics or hospitals with a gunshot wound.

It still stung that Matt had hit his mark and saved Trace's life. That made him beholden to the man. He couldn't be mad that it had happened. Not when it meant he might be dead now if Matt hadn't followed and fired when he had. Who knew his half brother was such a good shot? Hell, he didn't know a whole lot about the man who was his father's firstborn son. If only he hadn't been the man Lily had fallen in love with. Trace wasn't sure he could ever be cordial to him, knowing he was the one Lily had chosen over him.

And it burned him up that Matt had disavowed loving Lily. How could he make her fall in love with him and then leave her when she thought he would marry her? All these years, Trace had thought Lily had mar-

ried the love of her life. He'd tried to be content with
the thought that she was happy and well taken care of.
Even if he wasn't the love of her life, he'd wanted her
to be safe. All this time, she'd been alone.

And she hadn't let him know.

Still…she'd responded to his kiss. There was something there.

Was it enough?

Did she care enough about him to want to give them
a second chance?

Trace wrapped his mother in his arms and squeezed
her until she quit shaking. "Mom, I'm all right." He
held her at arm's length and smiled. "See? I'm perfectly fine."

She looked up at him and frowned. "No, you aren't.
Did the bullet graze your cheek? Do I need to take you
to the hospital?"

Someone snorted somewhere behind him.

Trace glanced over his shoulder to see Matt checking the fuel level on one of the tractors. He didn't care
if Matt thought he was a mama's boy. His mother meant
a lot to him, and she'd suffered a huge shock with the
death of her husband. "I'm okay, Mom. It's just a scratch
I got out in the field."

"I punched him, Mrs. Travis," Matt said. "The cut
on his cheek has nothing to do with the shooter." He
glanced down at his bruised knuckles. "I'm sorry if
that distresses you. I'll understand if you don't want
me to stay."

Trace's mother's frown deepened as she glanced
from Matt to Trace and back. "No. No. I'm sure there
was a good reason for you two to argue. I'm sure it has
to do with the woman calling the sheriff as we speak."

Trace's eyes narrowed as he stared down at his mother. "What do you know about it?"

She patted his chest. "That you better not get your-self shot." His mother hugged him close and then stepped free of his arms. "I have dinner ready whenever you're done here. Lily and I fed the animals, so all you need to do is wash up and come inside. Now, if you'll excuse me, I have rolls in the oven." She turned and rushed back into the house.

"Your mother has spunk," Irish said. "And something smells good. I could eat a horse."

On cue, a horse whinnied from the barn.

Irish's eyes widened.

"Watch what you say around the livestock," Trace warned. "We only raise the most intelligent horses on Whiskey Gulch Ranch." He said it with a straight face.

Irish chuckled and then frowned. "You're kidding, right?"

Trace raised his eyebrow in response. Then he turned away. "Mom's a good cook. Better hurry if you want to eat." Trace headed for the house and the two women who meant the most to him. Over his shoulder, he said, "That includes you, Hennessey."

The two men followed him into the house and washed their hands in the downstairs bathroom. The table was set with five place settings. In the center lay a platter of crispy fried chicken and another of roasted potatoes.

Lily entered the room and took a seat next to Matt. "The sheriff will be here in ten minutes."

"I'll set a plate for him." Trace's mother jumped up from the table and brought another place setting.

They settled in, passing the platters around the table.

Once they all had food on their plates, his mother said, "Okay, fill me in on what happened."

Trace gave her an abbreviated version of what had happened, leaving out the fight with Matt. He ended with "We finished the mowing. As hot as it's been, the hay should be dry enough to bale tomorrow."

"I don't want you all going out tomorrow. It's too dangerous," his mother said.

"We've got this, Mom," Trace said. "We were a little distracted today, but it won't happen again."

"If you insist on going, we're all going," his mother said.

Trace stiffened. "You need to stay home, where it's safe."

"I'm not staying locked in the house because someone is attacking my family," his mother said. "I know how to use a gun. Besides, we need all the help we can get to bale and store the hay before that storm system gets here sometime over the next couple of days. Roy called and said he'd be back tomorrow to help. He can drive the truck and also provide some backup, even if he can't do much in the way of heavy lifting."

Trace didn't like it, but his mother was still in charge, as far as he was concerned, even if his father had left him and Matt with the ranch. "Okay, but you're staying inside a vehicle."

"Deal," she said with a smirk. "I'll stay inside the cab of the tractor while I'm running the baling machine."

"I'll run the baling machine," Trace said.

His mother snorted. "Not if you want to get those bales loaded and stored. Unless you want me to toss eighty-pound bales up onto the back of the trailer." She raised her eyebrows and waited for his response.

"No. I'll toss bales. You can drive the baler, since you know how to run it."

She wouldn't be inside the house, but being in the enclosed cab of the tractor was better than nothing. Irish would have to be on his toes while the rest of them were busy loading the bales onto the trailer.

They were halfway through the meal when the sheriff showed up to take their statements. He accepted Mrs. Travis's invitation to join them, eating only a little before he got to work.

Trace, Irish and Matt took him out to where they'd been mowing so that he could see the tracks in the dirt, not that it would help much. The ground was dry, the wind had lifted some of the dust and deposited it into the grooves left by the four-wheeler's tires.

By the time they returned, dusk had settled over the land, making it difficult to distinguish anything in the shadows.

The sheriff promised to ask around for anyone who showed up at the clinics or hospitals nearby with a gunshot wound. He'd also check with the neighbors to see if any of them showed signs of wounds. Other than that, they had no other leads.

Once the sheriff left, Trace entered the house. He didn't want to admit to himself he was looking for Lily…but he was.

He didn't find her in the living room or the kitchen, so he climbed the stairs and hovered outside her door. With no real need to talk to her, he reasoned he could fill her in on their visit with the sheriff. With that excuse in mind, he knocked on her door.

No answer. He knocked again.

"She's out in the barn, checking on the animals," his mother said from behind him.

He forced a casual shrug. "I thought I'd fill her in on what the sheriff had to say."

His mother's lips quirked in an almost smile. "You can fill me in."

He told her the information in a few short sentences.

His mother frowned. "Is that all he can do?"

"We don't know who was after us, only that he rode an ATV and wore a helmet," Trace concluded.

His mother nodded. "Thank you. Now, go find Lily. I don't like the idea of her out in the barn alone." The older woman held up her hand. "I told her not to go out without a buddy."

"And she listened?" Trace shook his head. "She never listened to me, either."

"What happened between you and Lily?" his mother asked, her tone soft and whispered.

"I don't know. Ask her," he said and moved past his mother. If he knew, he might have fixed it way back when whatever it was happened in the first place. Now it was too late.

Or was it?

LILY WAS ON her way out to the barn when a voice called out.

"Lily?"

Lily turned to find Matt leaning against his motorcycle, his gaze on her. She altered her direction, aiming directly for him, anger spiking. "What the heck did you say to Trace to make him mad enough to hit you?"

"I only told him the truth," Matt said. "I told him that I never loved you like that. And for that I got slugged in the face." He rubbed at the bruise on his cheek. His eyes narrowed. "Trace was under the impression that you and I were getting married. Where did he get an idea like that?"

The anger drained out of her and Lily's shoulders sagged. "It's a long story."

"I have a few minutes. I'd like to hear it." Matt crossed his arms over his chest.

Lily glanced out at the horses grazing peacefully in the pasture and wished she could be as calm as they were. "I couldn't ruin his military career before it even began." She glanced back at Matt. "I was afraid that if he was associated with me, he wouldn't have passed the background check."

Matt frowned. "So what did that have to do with me?"

Lily looked again at the horses. "I had to do something that would make him leave me and not look back. Something that would break our connection so finally, no one would think we were ever together or had a chance of getting back together."

"So you used me," Matt stated.

Lily's chin dipped. "Yes. And I'm sorry. I told him that I was dumping him because I'd fallen in love with you."

A smile quirked the corners of his lips. "And that's such a bad thing?"

She glanced up into his face. "Of course not. But to anyone else in town, it might have appeared to be. Not that this is news to you, but you were the biggest bad-ass in Whiskey Gulch. Everyone would expect someone like me to be with someone like you. Not Trace."

Again, Matt rubbed his cheek. "So, you told him you

were busting up with him to marry me." He shook his head. "No wonder he was mad. You must have meant a lot to him if he's still mad after all these years. And that would explain why you came over to my house out of the blue to watch television and why you took a photo of the two of us sitting on my couch."

Lily grimaced. "Yeah, about that…"

Matt held up a hand. "Don't worry about it."

"I'm sorry I used you," Lily said.

"What I don't understand is why you haven't set the record straight."

Lily stared down at her feet. "I guess in the back of my mind, I'd hoped he would come back and fight for me. When he didn't, I listened to his mother's accounts of how well he was doing in the army, going from a soldier to Delta Force in such a short amount of time. He was a hero. He was much better off without me. I couldn't regret my decision to let go."

"You underestimate yourself," Matt said. "You aren't your parents."

She gave him a weak smile. "No. But…"

Matt nodded. "I get it. Reputations are hard to overcome, whether they are earned or inherited."

Lily frowned up at Matt. "You won't tell him any of this, will you?"

"Of course not," Matt said. "But you should. Seriously. Tell him."

Lily shook her head. "It's too late for us. Eleven years is a long time. Enough time to get over someone."

Matt tipped her chin up. "Are you over him?"

Lily's bottom lip trembled, and a single tear rolled down her cheek. She wanted to kick herself for letting her emotions show. Especially to this man.

Matt snorted softly and brushed the tear away with his thumb. "I guess that answers my question."

Lily's eyes widened. "Please, don't tell him."

"Hey." Matt stared down into her eyes. "Your secret is safe with me. My lips are sealed."

Lily flung her arms around his neck and hugged him tightly. "Thank you. Thank you, Matt."

"Don't mention it," Matt said. "Promise me that the next time you embroil me in one of your lies, at least clue me in. I don't mind getting punched in the face as long as I know the reason why."

Lily reached up and brushed her finger across the bruise. "I'm really sorry about that. I promise I won't do that again."

Matt looked over her shoulder and grimaced. "Well, we might have inadvertently done it again."

Lily's heart skipped several beats as she turned to find Trace standing behind her as she stood in Matt's arms.

With a sly grin, Matt leaned down and pressed a kiss to Lily's forehead. "This one's for me." Then he left her standing there and walked by Trace, bumping his shoulder accidentally on purpose as he passed.

Trace's face could have been set in stone as hard as his jaw was set. Lily recognized the tic in his cheek indicating just how angry he was. She'd seen it only when he was beyond angry with his father. Now he was mad at her.

Heat filled her cheeks. She refused to give in to her desire to excuse what he'd just witnessed. He didn't own her and had no right to tell her who she could or could not hug—or kiss, for that matter. Squaring her shoulders, she spun and walked toward the barn without uttering a comment. Maybe he would be mad enough to leave her alone.

That wasn't to be. Footsteps behind her made her very aware that he was following her. The roar of a motorcycle engine reminded her of what Trace had just witnessed between her and Matt.

Good. Let him stew on that image.

"What kind of boyfriend leaves his girlfriend to walk into a barn alone?" Trace said. "Especially into a barn where she'd been attacked before. Recently."

Lily didn't bother to turn around. "He's not my boyfriend."

"At one point, you thought he was. You thought he was close enough that he was going to marry you."

She entered the barn, turning only her head to say over her shoulder, "Apparently, I was wrong."

"So wrong that he never considered marrying you. Or even considered you as his girlfriend."

"Yeah, well," she said, "my bad."

Trace grabbed her arm and spun her around to face him. "Look, I don't like being lied to and I don't like being made to look like a fool."

Anger stung her chest. "If that's all it was to you, my apologies for making you look bad." She yanked her arm free and turned away from him, crossing the barn as quickly as she could, putting distance between them.

"Lily Davidson, we're not done talking," Trace boomed.

"Yes, we are," she said. "We were done talking eleven years ago." She swallowed hard on the lump in her throat, refusing to look at him, afraid that if she did, her love and disappointment would be all too evident in her eyes. She marched toward the steps leading up into the loft.

"What if someone's up there waiting to hit you again?" Trace asked.

"Then I guess I'll get hit." She didn't slow, too angry and sad to slow. Maybe being hit in the head wouldn't hurt as bad as the pain in her heart. Lily didn't care if someone was up there. That someone could put her out of her misery once and for all.

No one was there, but the shadows were deep and dark. She reached for her cell phone, but she'd left it on the counter in the kitchen. Without her cell phone, she didn't have a handy flashlight to find her way around in the dark loft. Too stubborn to go back down and admit to Trace she'd forgotten something as essential as a flashlight, Lily inched her way toward the back of the loft, searching for the stack of hay where Patches had hidden her kittens.

Was that sound someone moving in the darkness? Her gut tightened. She should have brought a flashlight. A heavy one she could use as a weapon.

A click sounded behind her.

Lily jumped and stifled a scream.

Chapter Eleven

"It helps to have a flashlight when you come up into a dark loft," Trace's voice said behind her, and the beam of a flashlight cut through the darkness.

Lily pressed a hand to her chest to calm her wildly beating heart. "I don't need your help," she muttered.

"Maybe not, but you need the light."

Lily didn't want to agree with him, so she didn't say anything at all. She did need the light if she wanted to snag the mama cat and get the kittens moved before they stacked more hay in the barn the next day. She continued on her quest to find the cat and her kittens.

When she reached the stack of hay, Lily pulled from her back pocket an old pillowcase she'd found in a cupboard in the house.

"Is that for the kittens?" Trace asked.

She shook her head. "No. The kittens won't be a problem. Patches was a feral cat that made her home in the barn. Catching her will be the challenge. Holding her will be even more of a task." She held up the pillowcase. "The pillowcase is for her."

"I'll get the cat," Trace said.

"No," Lily said, shaking her head. "She's more used to me than you."

Trace took the pillowcase from Lily. "Do you have to argue about everything?" His lips twitched. "I've got this." He shoved the flashlight at her. "Blind her with the light. Ready?"

No. Lily wasn't ready. She wasn't even sure how this would play out. Before she could utter a protest, he leaned over the top of the haystack. "Shine the light," he commanded.

Lily leaned over the hay and shone the light down into Patches's eyes.

The cat stared up at her, blinking in the sudden glare.

Trace didn't hesitate. He shoved his hand down into the gap, snagged the cat by the back of her neck and pulled her out of her cubby.

Patches screamed, yowled and fought to be free, twisting and cavorting, sinking her claws into Trace's arm and wrist.

He shook out the pillowcase and placed her down into it.

Lily grabbed the top of the case and closed it tightly.

Inside the case, Patches howled, scratched and hissed.

Blood dripped from several wounds on Trace's arm.

"You're hurt," Lily said.

"Doesn't matter," Trace said, his voice clipped. "I've got the cat. You get the kittens. We need to turn this one loose before she hurts herself or her milk dries up from stress."

With the flashlight in hand, Lily eased into the nesting area and gathered kittens one at a time until she had all five tucked into the pockets of her jersey jacket.

All the while they mewed for their mama and she called back.

Trace was halfway down the steps to the loft when Lily slipped over the haystack and started his way. She snagged a section of hay from a broken bale and hurried toward the stairs.

"Tack room?" Trace called out.

"Yes," she said and hurriedly descended to the ground. Lily passed Trace and opened the tack room door, holding it until Trace came through carrying his wriggling sack of angry cat. Once he was in, she shoved the door closed with her foot.

"I'll hold her until you get the kittens situated," he said.

Lily found a corner of the tack room behind the file cabinet that wasn't visible from the door and would be out of the way, where no one would accidentally step on the kittens. She spread the section of hay on the ground, added a saddle blanket and then eased the kittens out of her pockets, laying them one by one on the warm, soft blanket. Their eyes still closed, they scooted around on the blanket, desperately seeking their mama.

Lily straightened and dusted the hay from her jeans. "You can let Patches go."

Holding the pillowcase at arm's length, he chuckled. "Uh, yeah. We'll see how that goes." He gently laid the bag on the floor and let go of the top.

For a moment the bag lay completely still.

Then Patches shot out of the opening like a bullet out of a gun. She raced frenetically around the room, testing every corner for a path to escape. Finally, she hid beneath the back corner of the desk.

"I'm going to duck out for a bowl of water and cat food," Lily said, wishing she'd done it before they'd let

Patches loose. "Think you can keep her from getting through the door while it's open?"

Trace raised his eyebrows and snorted. "I'll do the best I can. No guarantees. She's mad and scared." He grabbed the pillowcase from the floor, positioned himself in front of the door and held it up like a red cape in front of a bull. "Go," he said.

Lily darted through the door, quickly closing it behind her. She found the water and food dish where she usually fed the cat, filled them and returned to the tack room. Knocking lightly, she waited for Trace's response.

"Make a run for it," he said through the thick paneling.

Stacking the water bowl on top of the food bowl, she freed one hand to open the door. Lily entered, careful not to slosh water into the food. Once inside, she closed the door with her foot and set the bowls on the ground. "Has she come out yet?"

"No." Trace wadded the pillowcase. "She won't until she's calmed down. Hopefully, it won't take long. The kittens are hungry and telling her about it."

Lily checked on the kittens. They were mewing softly, nudging at the blanket in search of their mother. "The sooner we leave her alone, the better off she is."

Trace nodded and headed for the door. With his hand on the knob, he waited for Lily to join him. "On three," he said. "One…two…" He jerked open the door, shoved her through and closed it quickly as a flash of fur raced toward them.

Lily gasped and ducked out of the way while Trace slammed shut the door.

Collapsing against the door, Lily laughed. "All that for a cat." She laughed until she held on to her sides.

Trace chuckled. The chuckle turned into a laugh and soon he was holding on to his sides.

When they finally slowed, Lily noticed the streaks of blood on his arm. "We need to take care of those scratches. We can't have you getting cat scratch fever."

"I'll be all right. They aren't bad. Just flesh—"

"Wounds," she finished for him. "How many times did you say that when you were on a mission?" Her smile faded and she stood in front of him, her heart hurting. So many times, she wondered where he was on the other side of the world. She'd wondered if he was all right, if someone was shooting at him, if he would live to come back to Whiskey Gulch. Her vision blurred with the tears she'd refused to shed. "Let's get you inside. There's antiseptic ointment in the downstairs medicine cabinet."

He allowed her to lead the way to the house and into the bathroom, where his mother kept a first-aid kit.

Slowly, painstakingly, Lily cleaned and dressed his wounds, smearing soothing ointment over the injury, then covering the larger ones with adhesive bandages.

When she was finished, she couldn't bring herself to look him in the eye. If she did, he'd know just how much touching him had affected her.

Matt's words came back to her.

Tell him.

That she loved him? That she'd lied to get him to leave Whiskey Gulch Ranch and join the military?

No. She couldn't. If he'd loved her as much as he'd said he'd loved her, he would have cared enough to fight for her.

Lily left the bathroom and hurried up the stairs to her room. Lost in her thoughts, she didn't hear footsteps behind her. She'd almost made it to her room, when Trace stopped her.

"Why?" he asked. The one word echoed within her soul.

"This isn't going to work," she whispered.

Trace's brow furrowed. "What isn't going to work?"

"As soon as we get the hay put up, I'm out of here," Lily said.

He tipped her chin up. "Is that really what you want to do?"

As he raised her chin, she lowered her eyelids. "Yes."

"Look at me, Lily," he said.

The warmth of his breath brushed against her cheek. She looked up at him. "What do you want from me?"

His lips turned up at the corners. "A kiss."

She shook her head. "No. I'm not going to ask you to kiss me," Lily stated, lifting her chin slightly.

"Are you sure?" He lowered his head until his lips hovered over hers, only a breath away.

"I'm sure—" Her voice caught in her throat as their breaths mingled.

Kissing Trace would be a huge mistake. But she wanted it more than she wanted to breathe.

"Do you want me to kiss you?" he asked.

Though she shook her head no, her mouth said, "Yes."

"Tell me, Lily," he urged. "Tell me you want me to kiss you."

"I don't—" Finally, her gaze met his and she recognized the desire in his eyes that matched the fire burning deep in her core. "Oh, hell," she muttered. "Who am I kidding?" She rose up on her toes and brushed her lips across his.

Trace leaned back, shaking his head. "Uh-uh," he said. "Not until you say the words."

Anger heated by desire made her words harsh. "All right, damn it. I want you to kiss me."

Trace gathered her close and lowered his head slowly, taking her lips in the most gentle and tender kiss she'd ever experienced.

Anger, need and desire bubbled up inside Lily. She didn't want the kiss to be tender. She wanted it hard, fast and deep, reminding her she was alive, and he was with her. After all these years, their bodies still remembered each other. She melted against him.

He pushed her up against the wall.

Lily wrapped her arms around him and pulled him impossibly closer. A kiss was not enough. She wanted him inside her. Wrapping her calf around his, she rubbed her center against his thigh and whispered against his lips, "I want more."

"Are you certain?"

"Yes," she breathed.

His lips left hers as he bent and scooped her up in his arms. Trace fumbled with the door handle.

Lily brushed his hand aside, twisted the knob and pushed open the door.

Trace carried her across the threshold and kicked the door closed behind them. He crossed the room in three easy strides and lowered her legs to the ground slowly. Then he gathered her close, kissing her hard and deep.

Lily had wanted this for so long. Her pulse hammered against her eardrums as she reached for the buttons on his shirt. She fumbled with one, two, three buttons.

Impatient, Trace yanked the hem from his waistband and pulled open his shirt, popping the remaining buttons free.

Lily laughed, dragging her blouse over her head and tossing it to the corner.

They worked in a frenzy, shedding clothing. He helped her, she helped him. They helped each other until they both stood naked at the foot of the bed.

"Sweet Lily, you're even more beautiful now than I remember," he said, his voice low, resonant and warm on her naked skin.

She smoothed a hand over his broad shoulders. "You got taller...and bigger." Her gaze slipped over his broad chest and down to his narrow waist and lower still to where the evidence of his desire jutted out prominently.

He cupped her cheek and stared down into her eyes. "Are you sure this is what you want? All you have to do is say no, and I'll walk away."

Lily's belly tightened. "No way. I want this." She'd been waiting so long for this moment. Trace had been her first. And he didn't know it, but he'd been her only.

Still, she wasn't a fool. "What about protection?"

He dived for the jeans he'd left crumpled on the floor, pulled his wallet out of his back pocket and unearthed a foil packet. He held it up with a grin.

Lily raised an eyebrow. "Just one?"

"There's more in my room," he said.

She nodded. "Good to know." Lily slid a hand along his cheek and to the back of his neck. She pulled him down to kiss her.

As they kissed, he backed her up until her legs

touched the mattress. Then he eased her down until she lay across the bed, her legs dangling over the side. Using his knees, he parted her thighs, stepping between. When he leaned over her, she wrapped her arms around him and pulled him close for a kiss.

His tongue thrust past her teeth to hers, caressing it in a long, sensuous glide. Then he left her lips and trailed his lips across her cheek and down the long column of her neck to where her pulse beat frantically at the base.

Lily trailed her fingers across his shoulders, loving the feel of his hard muscles encased in smooth skin.

Trace's mouth seared a path over her collarbone and down to her right breast. With his tongue he flicked her nipple and then rolled it between his teeth.

Lily arched her back off the mattress, urging him to take more. Take it all.

He sucked that breast into his mouth as deeply as he could, pulling hard.

Gasping, Lily's breath caught in her lungs and her core tightened.

He played that breast until she thought she would come apart in a million pieces. Then he moved to the other and performed the same teasing, flicking nips.

Lily thrashed against the mattress, her desire growing at an exponential rate. She wanted all of him. "Please," she cried.

He chuckled. "Please what?"

"Foreplay…is…overrated."

His chest pressed against her torso. When he chuckled again, the rumble vibrated through her. Abandoning her left breast, he trailed his tongue and lips across her ribs and down her flat abdomen, dipping his tongue into her belly button. As he neared the juncture of her thighs, he slowed, then paused.

Lily held her breath, willing him to take her there. Take her with his fingers, with his tongue, with his staff.

Trace cupped her sex and dipped a finger into her wet channel.

Oh, sweet heaven…take me, she thought.

As if he'd heard her, his fingers parted her folds and he blew a warm stream of air over that heated strip of flesh.

Lily bunched the comforter in her fists.

His finger slid up inside her.

Lily moaned.

"Oh, baby, I've only just begun," Trace said, his breath warm against the inside of her thighs. He touched her there.

An explosion of sensations roiled over her. Her hands flew from the comforter to his hair, weaving through the strands to pull him closer. "Trace!" Lily cried.

"Does that mean you like it?" he asked. "Or do you want me to stop?"

"Don't," she gasped. "Don't stop."

He touched his tongue to her again.

Lily arched off the mattress. "It's good. Oh, so good."

Trace flicked and laved her there until she writhed beneath him, beyond her senses. She couldn't think, couldn't see, couldn't breathe. A ripple of electricity started at her core and spread like wildfire along her nerves, working its way outward to her very fingertips. Wave upon wave of sensations washed over her. She rode the wave all the way to the end. As she drifted back to earth, she collapsed against the mattress, dragging in deep gulps of air. Even after she got her breathing under control, that ache deep down continued. She threaded her hands in his hair and pulled. "I want you. Now."

Trace moved up her body, climbing up between her legs to claim her lips with his. He tasted of her.

Lily moaned against his mouth as Trace touched her entrance with the tip of his shaft.

She gripped his buttocks in an attempt to bring him home.

"Not yet." He leaned up on one arm, grabbed the foil packet, tore it with his teeth.

Lily took it from him, pulled out the protection and rolled it over his engorged staff.

Then Trace kissed her and pressed into her damp channel.

Impatient, Lily grabbed his hips and pulled him all the way into her.

Trace inhaled deeply and let out the air slowly as he gave her time to adjust to his girth. "Lily, you feel so good."

"Mmm," she murmured.

Trace settled into a steady rhythm, pumping in and out of her.

With her hands gripping his hips, she encouraged him to go faster, pump harder.

He moved through her slick center with ease, his thick member stretching her deliciously. His pace increased until finally he slammed into her and he held steady, his shaft pulsing with his release.

Lily's fingers dug into his backside, holding him close.

When at last he relaxed, he fell down on top of her, rolled them both onto their sides and held her there.

Lily pressed her cheek against his chest. Tears slipped from her eyes. She swallowed hard to keep from sobbing aloud. This was what she'd been waiting for. He was who she'd waited for. But making love didn't solve anything. It only complicated matters.

Chapter Twelve

Trace felt the dampness of her tears against his skin. His heart squeezed hard inside his ribs. "Lily."

She shook her head and raised a hand, touching a finger to his lips. "Don't." The one word came out thick with emotion.

"But, Lily, we have to talk," he insisted.

"Not tonight," she said.

"Then tomorrow."

She didn't answer. Lily lay in his arms, her body pressed against his.

He didn't want the night to end. He was afraid that when it did, she would slip from his arms forever. Trace couldn't let that happen. Not again.

Lily draped a leg over his and an arm across his chest. Soon her body relaxed against his, and her breathing deepened. She'd fallen asleep.

Trace lay for a long time, staring up at the ceiling, wanting to wake her and force her to talk to him. He wanted her to tell him why she'd said she was going to marry Matt, when in fact she'd had no intention of doing so. Had she been afraid of leaving her home? Had she not wanted to be a military wife? Had she been afraid of marrying a man who put himself in harm's way?

She lay so peacefully that Trace couldn't bring himself to wake her.

Eventually, he fell into a troubled sleep. He woke in the cool, gray light of predawn and stared around at the walls, trying to get his bearings. He wasn't in his room.

The previous night came back to him in a flood of memories. He rolled over in the full-size bed, already knowing but needing to verify that Lily was already gone.

He threw back the sheets and swung his legs out of the bed.

Damn. How had she left the room without waking him? He was in her room, for Pete's sake. How had she dressed and then opened and closed the door without him hearing a thing?

He gathered his clothes, dressed quickly and pulled on his boots. When he stepped outside the door of her bedroom, he paused and listened. Sounds of people moving about came from downstairs. His mother would already be up, cooking breakfast for everyone. Had Lily gone down to help her?

Trace ducked into his room and changed his shirt for one with long sleeves. Hauling hay was a dirty, itchy task if one didn't cover as much bare skin as possible. The more he covered, the less he'd be poked and stabbed by the strands of hay. He crossed the hallway to the bathroom, splashed water on his face, combed his hair and brushed his teeth. When he was finished, he hurried downstairs to the kitchen.

Irish stood at the counter, buttering toast. Matt was at the coffee maker, pouring fresh brew. Roy hobbled through the back door on his damaged foot and called out, "Good morning."

Trace's mother manned the stove, scrambling eggs.

There was no sign of Lily.

"Good morning, sleepyhead," his mother sang. "Grab a cup of coffee. Breakfast is about ready. If you're looking for Lily, she just stepped out to go to the barn to check on the cat."

"I offered to go with her," Irish said. "But she insisted she would only be a minute."

"She was stepping into the barn when I drove up," Roy said.

His gut clenched. Did she not understand the danger of going out by herself? "I'll go check on her." Trace exited through the back door. He'd made it to the top of the porch steps when he saw her striding toward him from the barn.

She didn't appear to be harmed in any way.

Trace breathed a sigh of relief.

She met his gaze only briefly. "Patches was confined to the tack room all night and will be there all day until we get the hay put up. I fashioned a litter box out of an old, shallow box and filled it with dirt and gravel so that she can relieve herself. Otherwise, there was no telling what she'd do to that tack room."

"Good thinking," Trace said.

When she went to pass him, he snagged her arm. "Lily."

She paused but still didn't look up at him.

"Oh, there you two are," his mother called out from the porch. She turned and reentered the house.

Trace looked down at Lily. "We will talk."

She nodded.

Trace released her arm and Lily ran up into the house.

For a long moment, Trace stared up at the house. What had changed from last night to this morning? Or had nothing changed, and he hadn't recognized a problem remained between the two of them?

Who was he kidding? Sex didn't solve anything. It just made the situation more complicated. By the time Trace entered the house and kitchen, everyone else was seated and talking about the day ahead.

Already they were making assignments of who would do what.

Lily would drive the tractor with the rake, piling the dried straw into neat rows. His mother would follow on the baler. Roy would drive the truck that would pull the trailer. Trace and Matt would load the rectangular bales onto the trailer while Irish rode around the hayfield protecting them from potential attacks.

"We'll have to move quickly," Roy said.

Lily nodded. "The storm headed our way has picked up some speed and will get here sooner than previously anticipated. It's expected to hit late this afternoon." She picked up her plate of half-eaten food and carried it to the sink. "I'll be out at the barn when you are ready."

"I'm done," Irish said. "I'll go with you."

Lily waited by the back door for Irish to stow his plate and glass in the sink and grab his hat.

They were gone by the time Trace finished his breakfast and cleared his place setting from the table. When he reached the barn, he found Irish and Lily loading fuel into the tractors from the large tank positioned several yards from the outbuildings.

When Lily finished pumping fuel into the large tractor, she climbed aboard and moved it to where implements were lined up against a fence.

Trace followed.

Lily backed the tractor up to the baler, and Trace attached the baler to the three-point hitch. When all the mechanics were working correctly, Lily drove the tractor to the gate and parked. On the other tractor, Roy drove to where Trace stood among the implements. He backed the tractor up to the acreage rake, and Trace attached the tool to the second tractor. Roy parked the tractor behind the baler.

Trace's mother came out of the house dressed in jeans, with her hair pulled back in a braid, a hat shading her face, and carrying a large basket. She looked years younger. Trace could imagine the pretty girl his father met and fell for decades ago, and his heart hurt for the love lost. Rosalynn deposited the basket on the back seat of the pickup and climbed aboard the baling tractor.

Irish and Matt stood by the damaged ATV from the day before.

Matt shook his head. "I don't think this thing is going anywhere. Even if we could get it started, the frame's bent. It'll take a lot of work to get it straight again."

Irish's brow crinkled. "Well, what am I supposed to use to provide protection? Needs to be something that's not fully enclosed. A truck won't do."

Trace's lips twitched. "I don't suppose you ride horses, do you?"

Irish grimaced. "I have ridden, but it's been a long time."

"It's like riding a bicycle. Once you learn how, you never forget." Trace grinned.

Irish frowned. "Tell that to the horses. They seem to have a sixth sense about their riders' experience."

Lily came out of the barn leading a mare, saddled, bridled and ready to go. She approached Irish and patted the horse's neck. "This is Lady, one of our gentlest horses. She won't give you a bit of trouble."

Irish eyed the animal with suspicion and then glanced around at the others. His gaze landed on Roy. "I don't suppose—"

Roy raised his hands. "Don't ask me. I've got a bum foot. Can't keep it in the stirrup."

Irish shrugged and took the reins and handed his rifle to Trace. "Guess it's you and me, Lady." He placed his foot in the stirrup and swung his leg over the animal, landing hard in the saddle. Once he was settled, Trace handed him the rifle. Irish rested it across his thighs and gathered the reins in his hands.

Lady stood patiently without dancing around, like some horses had a habit of doing.

While Trace opened the gate, Lily climbed onto the tractor with the rake. Matt hopped into the bed of the pickup.

Trace's mother drove through first, followed by Lily, then Roy in the truck and Trace on foot. Once through the gate, Trace closed it and climbed up into the passenger seat of the pickup.

When they reached the mown field, Lily led the way, raking the hay into neat rows. Trace's mother followed behind the rake with the baler, making neat, rectangular bales and dropping them in the row.

Roy dragged the trailer behind the baler.

Matt and Trace tossed the bales onto the trailer, forming rows and then stacks as they went.

The day warmed into a sweltering heat. Sweat dripped off the men as they stacked bales.

Irish rode the perimeter of the field, rifle in hand, keeping a close eye on the shadows in the tree line. Knowing him, he wouldn't let the surprise attack of the day before happen again.

At noon, Rosalynn stopped her tractor and waved to Lily, indicating she should stop as well. The group gathered in the shade of the trees with the basket Trace's mother had stowed in the back seat of the pickup. It was full to the brim with fried chicken, sandwiches and potato chips.

Irish remained on guard until Trace finished his food.

When Trace was finished, he relieved Irish of his rifle and stood guard while Irish rested and ate.

Clouds built in the distance, an ominous dark wall moving their direction.

His mother moved to stand beside him, a frown puckering her smooth brow. "We need to get moving if we want to finish this field before that rain hits."

Trace nodded and turned to the others. "Saddle up. We have more work to do before we can call it a day."

"I'll be done raking soon," Lily said. "Then I can help stack bales."

Trace nodded. "We can use all the help we can get to load all those bales."

As soon as Lily finished raking the hay, she drove the tractor up to Trace. "I'm taking the tractor back to the barn."

"I'll go with you," Trace said. He called out to Matt, "I'm going with Lily to the barn. You got this for a few?"

Matt tossed a bale onto the trailer. "Got it."

"I can get to the barn and back by myself," Lily argued.

"I'd rather not risk it," Trace said and crawled up on the back of the tractor, hanging on to the back of her seat.

"Seriously, I'll be fine on my own," she muttered.

"The more you argue, the longer it will take." He waved a hand toward the barn. "Drive."

She shot a glance over her shoulder, her lips twisting. "Bossy much?"

He chuckled. "Only when I need to be." He winked.

"Better hold on, then." Lily's lips twitched into a brief smile before she popped the clutch and the tractor lurched forward.

Thankfully, Trace was holding on tightly, or he'd have been thrown off. "Hey, don't forget I'm back here."

She snorted. "Believe me, I didn't."

He liked when she was sassy. It reminded him of when they'd been teens and racing horses across the fields. Trace wished it could be like this all the time. He suspected they had some rough patches yet to overcome. He hoped they overcame them without ending their relationship. If he had his way, they'd skip over the trials and get right back to making love and teasing each other.

Yeah, and pigs could fly.

LILY HAD GOTTEN up early that morning and slipped out of the bed she'd shared with Trace. No matter how much she wanted to be with him, she realized physical attraction was not enough. She loved Trace more than she needed to breathe. But the fact was, he hadn't come back to fight for her.

After all the years of pining for him, Lily wanted more. She wanted a man who would move heaven and earth to be with her. A man who wasn't afraid to tell her how he felt and who wanted what she wanted, a lasting relationship that would weather any storm.

She stopped at the gate and waited until Trace dismounted from the tractor and opened it. Then she drove through, backed the hay rake into position next to the other tractor implements and waited while Trace unhooked the three-point hitch. Once he had it loose, she parked the tractor in the shed, where Trace's father had stored it.

Trace reached up, fitting his hands around her waist, and lifted her from the tractor seat, letting her slide down his torso until her feet brushed the ground. His hands remained around her waist.

Lily didn't want him to let go. She inhaled the scent of the outdoors, dried sweat and male. She'd missed him so much. Her body swayed toward him, ready to pick up where they'd left off the night before. For a moment she really considered it.

A rumble of distant thunder brought her back to reality. She straightened and stepped out of his grasp. "We'd better get back to the others." Did her voice sound disappointed? She hoped not, even if she felt it.

"Walking back?" he asked.

She shook her head. "You can walk. I'll ride." She entered the barn and strode to the first stall on the right. Dusty, the buckskin gelding, pawed at the stall door and whinnied when she drew near. "Hey, boy. Wanna stretch your legs?" She clipped a lead onto his halter and opened the stall door. The horse pushed through, nudging her shoulder to hurry. "All in due time," she assured him as she tied him to a hook on the wall.

Trace tossed a saddle blanket and her saddle over the animal's back.

"How did you know which one I use?" she asked.

"I remembered," he said, tightening the girth around Dusty's belly. "Things haven't changed much around here."

Other than his father's passing, Trace was right. The saddles they'd used as teens were still functional. What had changed was the people. Lily had grown up and Trace had moved on with his life in the army.

Lily left Trace to complete tightening the girth and eased into the tack room for a bridle.

Patches ducked her head around the corner of the filing cabinet. When she spotted Lily, she walked out, leaving her kittens mewing in protest. The cat weaved her body around Lily's legs and paused long enough for Lily to scratch her beneath the chin.

"How are your babies?" Lily asked.

Patches meowed and walked toward the door.

"I know you want out, but you'll have to wait a little longer." Lily checked the water and food dishes. They were still full and the litter box she'd fashioned out of a cardboard box was still unused. "Sorry, girl. We'll let you out as soon as we have the hay put up."

Grabbing a bridle from a nail on the wall, she squeezed through the door, shutting the cat inside.

"How's Patches and the kittens?" Trace took the bridle from Lily's hands.

"Patches is impatient, but the kittens are fine."

Trace slipped the bit between Dusty's teeth, looping the leather straps over his ears. Unhooking the lead from the animal's halter, he led the horse out of the barn and handed the reins to Lily. Then he bent and cupped his hands.

She could have gone straight for the stirrup. It was a stretch, but she'd done it many times before. Instead, Lily put her foot in his hands like she had all those years ago and swung her leg over the saddle.

Before she could slip her foot into the stirrup, Trace grabbed the saddle horn, stuck his boot into the stirrup and swung up behind her, landing lightly on the horse's rump, just behind the saddle's seat.

"You could have saddled your own horse," she said.

"Why?" he said, wrapping his arms around her waist. "This is much cozier."

Lily frowned and looked over her shoulder at him. "Back when we were young, you always made me ride in the back."

"I liked it when you wrapped your arms around me," he said. "But I find I like wrapping my arms around you even better."

Another rumble of thunder reminded them of the impending storm.

Trace stared into the distance at the dark clouds building on the horizon. "Much as I enjoy being alone with you, we'd better get back to the others. I'm thinking we have less than an hour before that storm hits."

Lily nudged the horse's flanks and reined him toward the open gate. Once they were through, Trace leaned down and pushed the gate closed.

Free of the barn and out in the open, Dusty took off, galloping across the field, his legs stretching out, eating the distance between the barn and the people working the hay.

Trace held on tightly around Lily's waist.

She loved the strength in his arms and the solid wall of muscles he pressed against her back. If only they didn't have to haul the hay, she'd keep riding, without a care for the future and what might happen next.

All too soon, they reached the others.

Rosalynn was just finishing baling the last row of loose straw. She parked the tractor at the end of the field and climbed down, walking toward the truck.

Lily aimed Dusty toward the tree line for a place to tie him up where he could be in the shade and still graze while they loaded hay.

After a brief squeeze, Trace slipped off the horse, landing nimbly on the ground. He held up his arms for Lily and helped her from the saddle.

Irish waved at them and nudged his horse toward where they were standing.

Trace took the reins from Lily and tied them to a low-hanging tree branch.

He was just turning back toward Lily when she heard a rustling in the trees.

Lily spun toward the sound and ducked low.

She couldn't see anyone moving in the shadows, but the rustling continued, and a loud snort sounded close by.

Her heart stopped. If that sound was what she thought it was, she had seconds to get the heck out of there.

"Run!" Trace yelled as he pulled the pistol from his holster and aimed it toward the spot where Lily stood.

For a nanosecond, Lily froze. Then she launched herself from the position where she had been standing and ran out into the open. The truck and tractor were too far for her to make it fast enough, so she ran toward a hay bale, wishing it were a heavy round bale instead of an eighty-pound rectangle that wouldn't provide any protection from what was hiding in the woods.

The sound of feet pounding against the ground behind her made Lily run faster.

Out of the corner of her eye, she saw Trace take careful aim.

The blast of a gunfire sounded.

Lily dived behind the hay bale and crouched, pulling her body in on all sides, out of sight of what was chasing her.

Another shot rang out and the sound of something crashing hard against the earth brought her head up and she dared to look over the top of the bale.

Lying in the dust and hay stubble was a gigantic feral hog with wicked tusks. It heaved a last breath and lay still with two gunshot wounds to the heart.

Lily collapsed against the bale, her knees trembling, her pulse still thundering through her system.

Trace hurried toward her, running past the hog to gather her into his arms. He held her for a long moment. "Are you okay?"

She nodded. "Thanks to you."

Irish rode up on Lady, his rifle in one hand, the other managing the reins. "Wow. That was some good shooting. That hog didn't look like he was going to stop for one tiny bullet." Irish slipped from the saddle and walked around the dead animal. "Should be some good eating. Anyone fancy ham for dinner?" He glanced at Lily. "You all right?"

She nodded from the reassuring comfort of Trace's arms. "I am."

"I would have fired the rifle, but you were in direct line of fire from where I stood. Trace had to get him, or…"

"Or the hog would have gotten me," Lily said softly.

"He didn't," Trace said and smoothed a hand over her hair. "And Irish is right. That hog will make good eating."

"That's right," Rosalynn said, joining them. "Better us eating him than him gouging one of us."

Matt trotted toward them from the direction of the truck and trailer. "You guys all right?"

"Yes," Trace assured him.

Irish grinned at Lily. "I've never seen anyone run so fast."

"A good thing she did. That hog wasn't far behind her," Matt said. "I'm glad he didn't catch up with you."

Irish winked. "That's right. We need all the help we can get loading the rest of that hay."

Lily appreciated that they all were rallying around her. But the wall of clouds was nearing, and they still had half a field to load onto the trailer and get to the barn before the skies opened up and dumped rain on them.

Another, louder rumble of thunder caught everyone's attention.

"We'd better get back to work," Rosalynn said. "Lily and I can stack the hay."

"Let's do this. We don't have much time," Trace said. "I can already smell the rain."

Lily sniffed the air. She, too, could smell the earthy dampness of the weather system moving toward them. She and Rosalynn climbed up on the back of the trailer.

Matt and Trace tossed the bales as high as they could, and Lily and Rosalynn moved them into neat rows, layering them carefully so they held in place as the layers grew higher. Trace threw the last bale up onto the trailer and climbed up after it. "We don't have time to tie it down. You two go on back to the barn. I'll ride back here with the hay to make sure nothing starts sliding off."

"We stacked it in crisscrossing layers," Rosalynn said. "It'll hold. Ride up front with Roy and Matt. I'll take the tractor."

"And I'll ride Dusty," Lily said. She didn't offer but left it open for Trace to suggest he ride double.

Trace frowned at the tall stack of hay. "If you're sure it'll hold, I'll go with Lily in case there's another hog hiding out in the underbrush."

Lily let go of the breath she hadn't realized she'd been holding and ducked her head to hide her smile. She was glad he would be riding double with her. Especially after he'd saved her from the charging hog.

Roy drove the truck and trailer to where the hog lay. Matt tied a rope around the animal's back legs and to the back of the trailer. They would drag it back to the barn, where they could field dress it and process it for the freezer.

Lily shivered as she passed the hog.

"You were smart," Trace said. "You moved fast."

Her lips pressed into a thin line. "I would not have been fast enough to outrun that thing," she said. "You're the reason I wasn't mauled or killed." She turned to him. "Thank you."

Trace pushed a hand through his hair, his gaze searching the undergrowth, as if expecting another feral hog to jump out. "I'm glad I was here, and that I had a gun."

"Me, too." Lily untied Dusty's reins from the tree branch and looped them over the saddle horn.

Trace cupped his hands and bent low.

"You know I can reach the stirrup, don't you?" she asked, her lips twisting in a wry grin.

He looked up at her, his face serious. "Humor me, will you? I almost lost you to a hog today." Not a smile curled the corners of his lips, and there was no twinkle of laughter in his eyes. The man appeared to be years older than he'd looked at the beginning of the day.

Lily nodded. "Okay, then." She placed her foot in his cupped hands and pushed up until she could swing her leg over the saddle.

She moved her leg back, giving him room to place the toe of his boot in the stirrup.

He swung up behind her.

"You could have ridden in the saddle," Lily said. "I don't mind riding behind."

"The stirrups are fitted to the length of your legs. Besides, I'd rather have your back as we return to the barn."

Lily frowned, her mind working through what he'd just said.

He had her back. Meaning, if someone shot at her, he'd get Trace first. Trace would take the bullet, instead of her.

Her hands tightened on the reins and her pulse sped. "Trace, I don't like—"

He leaned into her back, his lips brushing her earlobe. "Don't go getting your panties in a wad. Give the horse his head. He'll get us back to the barn in no time."

"But—"

Trace squeezed his legs against hers and dug his heels into the horse's flanks.

Dusty leaped forward, got the bit between his teeth and took off at a full gallop across the field, headed for the barn and his dinner.

Lily was glad the horse raced across the field. Maybe if he went fast enough, and with Irish bringing up the rear, they wouldn't take a bullet. Now that Trace was back, Lily didn't want anything to happen to him. Heck, the man had fought in the Middle East through several deployments. He couldn't die back in Texas on his own property. That would be all kinds of wrong. And Lily couldn't live knowing he was gone.

Chapter Thirteen

Trace held on to Lily as the horse loped across the field. They caught up with and passed the truck hauling the trailer full of hay and arrived at the barn with enough time to remove the saddle and run a quick brush over Dusty's sweaty coat before the others got back. Trace stepped out of the barn as Lily led the horse into a stall and the truck stopped in front of the barn.

Irish rode into the yard and slipped out of the saddle to stand on his feet. He squatted several times and rubbed his backside. "Those are some muscles I don't use that often," he said, grimacing.

Trace grinned. "I know how you feel. If you don't ride on a regular basis, one day in the saddle will make you sore for a week." He grabbed a bale of hay and carried it into the barn. Between him and Matt, they got started on unloading the trailer.

Lily joined in, carrying the eighty-pound bales a little slower, but she didn't complain or sit it out. She worked hard alongside the men.

Trace's mother entered the barn and started to lift a bale.

Trace took the bale from her hands. "Mom, you'd

serve an even greater purpose if you feed us when this is all done."

She nodded and touched a hand to the small of her back. "But that rain is almost here."

"If we have to, we can back the trailer into the barn to keep the hay dry," Trace said. "You've already helped more than you should."

"What you mean is *for an old woman*."

Trace shook his head. "You're anything but old. Still, you need to take a break. We can handle the rest."

"He's right, Rosalynn," Lily said as she grabbed another bale and carried it over to the foot of the stairs leading up to the loft. "We're going to be starving when we're done here."

"You should go help her," Trace said.

Lily snorted, her brow dipping. "And let you two have all the fun? No way." She came back for another bale. "I will, however, let you guys carry these bales up the stairs to the loft."

"Deal," Trace said. "Mom, let Irish walk you into the house. I know for a fact he's great at peeling potatoes."

"Hey, are you volunteering me for KP?" Irish stood in the open doorway to the barn. "I am pretty good at it." He grinned. "Then, at least, I won't have to stand out in the lightning." He tipped his head toward the southwest. "It's almost here. You have about fifteen minutes before the rain starts."

Lily carried bales to the bottom of the stairs while Matt and Trace took turns carrying them up into the loft. Working as a team, they had the trailer unloaded in less than twenty minutes. Lily carried the last bale into the barn as the sky opened up and rain poured down.

She stood at the door and sighed. Any way she

looked at it, if she stepped out of the barn, she'd be drenched in the first five steps. Getting to the house would be very wet.

Matt and Trace joined her at the door.

"We could wait until it lets up," Matt said.

Trace shook his head. "It's predicted to last all night. And I'm hungry." He patted his flat abdomen.

"Me, too." Lily rolled her aching shoulders. "We worked hard."

Matt grinned. "Got it done."

Trace glanced at the massive hog lying in the middle of the barn. "We might as well dress this hog. No use getting a shower until that's done."

"You'll need something to put the meat in." Lily grabbed an empty paper feed sack and lifted it over her head. "I'll be right back with containers and freezer paper."

"Grab an extra knife while you're at it," Trace said. "I'll watch until you get to the house." A crack of thunder rattled the rafters of the barn. "On second thought... you stay here. I'll go get what we need."

"I'm not afraid of a little lightning," Lily said, ready to go out into the storm. She didn't stand around arguing. Instead, she dashed out the door before Trace could grab her and insist on her staying in the barn.

"Damn it, Lily," Trace called out.

"I'll be right back," she said over her shoulder, sure he wouldn't hear her anyway. Not with the rain pounding down on the metal roof of the barn.

Considering she had been hot and sweaty by the time she'd finished unloading the trailer, she should be thankful for the drenching rain to cool her off. The only problem was being able to see as she ran through the deluge. When she finally made it to the porch, she stopped long enough to squeeze the water out of her hair. Too wet to enter the house, she poked her head through the back door and spotted Trace's mother at the stove. "Rosalynn."

The older woman spun, a spatula in her hand. "Oh, my goodness," she said. Turning the flame down beneath the pot simmering on the stove, she hurried over to where Lily dripped on the tile. "Come in, dear. You're not going to hurt the floor."

Lily shook her head. "I'd rather not. We're going to process the hog. I need supplies."

Rosalynn nodded. "I know just what you'll use." She hurried around the kitchen gathering items from drawers and the pantry, stuffing them in a large canvas bag. When she was finished, she returned to Lily. "Let me take it out there. You need to come in and get a shower."

With a smile, Lily relieved the woman of the bag. "No use you getting wet, too. We've got this. Between the three of us, we should be able to take care of things quickly." With the straps of the bag looped over her shoulder, Lily headed back the way she'd come, pausing briefly at the edge of the porch as a bright flash lit the darkness and an answering rumble of thunder rattled the eaves.

Taking a deep breath, she ran down the stairs and across the backyard to the barn. She didn't care that lightning struck nearby. She only wanted to be close to Trace.

TRACE AND MATT strung the hog from one of the rafters and started the process of rendering it for consumption.

They worked in silence.

Trace didn't want to like his half brother, but the man worked hard and efficiently, without complaint. And he was prior service. A marine.

"Why did you get off active duty?" Trace asked, curious about this man with whom he'd have to share the Whiskey Gulch Ranch or sell it.

"Injury," Matt said. "Wrecked my knee. I've since been given a new one, but medical boarded off active duty. Your—our father came to my rescue when I returned to Whiskey Gulch. I didn't know what I was going to do with my life without the military. I was good with car engines, but not much else. He set me up with my own shop, loaned me the money to get started and told me I could pay it back in my own time."

"Generous of him," Trace said. "He never wanted me to do anything but ranching. Blew a gasket when I announced I was going into the army."

"Should have gone into the marines," Matt said with a grin. "He might not have been as mad."

"Whatever," Trace muttered. "He liked to have control of his corner of the world."

"And you didn't like being controlled," Matt concluded.

"That about covers it." Trace worked the hide away from the hindquarters.

Matt helped by pulling back while Trace cut. "Was Lily one of James's control issues as well?"

Trace bristled. He didn't want to discuss Lily with this man. "Let's just say he didn't approve." His tone was deep and tinged with anger.

Matt held up his hands. "Sorry, dude. I didn't mean to stir the hornet's nest. But you need to know, there never was anything between me and Lily… We were friends. Only. She hung out with me for a week, came to my house once to watch a game, and once you were gone, she never came back to hang out."

Trace frowned. "Why would she tell me that she was marrying you?"

Matt shrugged. "Did you ask her?"

"No."

The other man chuckled. "Seems like that would be your first stop."

Trace snorted. "Getting a straight answer out of her can be a challenge."

"One worth taking on," Matt said. "She's a smart, hardworking and beautiful woman."

The more Matt talked, the more Trace wanted to punch him. He straightened, his eyes narrowing. "Look, she's—"

"Off-limits?" Matt shook his head. "Have you told her that? You're going to mess up and lose her if you don't do something about it. I think your boy, Irish, has a thing for her."

"Irish is harmless," Trace muttered and went back to work on the hide.

"Maybe he is. Maybe I don't know what I'm talking about." Matt pulled at the hide. "Irish himself said that Lily was just the kind of woman he'd want to marry." Matt lifted his shoulders. "He could have been kidding or just making a statement. Maybe you need to open your eyes to what's right there in front of you."

Trace looked up, his gaze seeking the barn door.

Lily entered, carrying a bag and drenched. Her blouse lay plastered to her body like a second skin and water dripped off her chin, nose and eyelashes.

Even as sodden as she was, she was beautiful in

Trace's eyes. And she stood right there in front of him, a smile pulling at her lips. "In case you didn't know, it's still raining out there."

Matt chuckled. "I think we know." He pointed at the roof the rain was hammering against.

"There's a towel in the tack room," Trace said. "You can let Patches out now. I'm sure she's ready." After his conversation with Matt, his words to her seemed…inadequate.

Lily dropped the bag at Trace's feet. "You made good progress in a short amount of time."

"This is the hard part," Matt said. "It won't take long, once we get going."

Lily disappeared into the tack room, leaving the door slightly open to allow Patches to make her escape.

Trace glanced that way every so often. Patches never came out. At least not while he was watching.

Lily came out patting her body with a ragged towel and squeezing her ponytail to get the water out. She studied their progress. Lily had been with Trace after he'd been hunting deer and had helped by wrapping the meat in butcher paper. The hog proved to be a lot more of an effort than a deer. But with three of them working together, they completed their work.

The worst of the lightning had moved past the house, but the rain continued to beat loudly against the roof.

Lily, Trace and Matt stepped out into nature's shower and let the rain wash away the dirt, hay and blood.

"I can't remember when I've been more exhausted or covered in blood," Lily said.

"I can," Matt said, his tone flat, his gaze on the horizon.

Trace knew exactly how Matt felt. He'd been involved in some bloody battles during his time with Delta Force. But this was Texas, not Afghanistan or Iraq. They'd have good meat in the freezer to last through the winter. If he stayed.

"We got a lot done," Trace said. "Now there's hay to see the horses through the winter."

Matt nodded. "And meat for the freezer, enough to feed whoever lives on the ranch."

"We'll have to wait until the other field dries before we can cut the hay for the big round bales needed to get the cattle through the winter. But that effort won't require tossing bales onto a trailer."

Lily raised her hands in the air and stretched, wincing. "Thankfully, all of that can be done by tractors, not human backs."

"It will still require a lot of work and we haven't checked the fences in a while."

"I can help with that tomorrow," Matt said.

"Don't you have engines to fix?" Lily asked.

"I'll work on them tonight." Matt's lips twisted. "That's what shop lights are for. Fencing needs daylight."

Trace wanted to hate the man who was his father's firstborn son, but he couldn't. Matt had worked as hard as he had that day. He'd served his country, and he cared about Lily and Trace's mother. Not that Trace had appreciated his advice on how to handle Lily. But the man's words roiled around in his head, refusing to be ignored.

"I bet Mom's got something amazing ready for dinner," Trace said. "We'd better get cleaned up."

Trace took Lily's hand and walked with her to the house, rain dripping down his face and into his eyes. He

wanted anyone watching to know that she was important to him. The Irishes and Matts of the world would
have to back off or suffer his wrath. If he could convince her, Lily was his and he wouldn't let her go again.
Not without a fight.

Chapter Fourteen

Lily was first in the shower, rinsing quickly, know-ing there were two others who needed hot water to get clean. When she was finished, she dried off quickly, wrapped a towel around her hair and another around her body, and stepped out into the hallway.

Right into a solid wall of muscles.

"Oh," Lily said, her hand rising to rest on Trace's damp chest.

He was barefoot, wearing only a pair of jeans, and he was clean.

Lily frowned. "You had a shower?"

He tipped his head toward the master bedroom at the end of the hallway. "I used Mom's shower." His gaze swept over her bare shoulders, his pupils dilat-ing. "Feel better?"

She nodded, her cheeks heating. The only thing be-tween her and his hands was the fluffy white towel. She didn't look up into his eyes, afraid he'd see just how excited she was by his nearness. "Much better. What about Matt? Did he want to jump in?"

"He grabbed a plate to go and left."

Lily frowned. "Was it something we said?"

Trace smiled. "No. He had work to do at his shop."

He tipped her chin up, forcing her to look at him. "Thank you."

"For what?"

"You were amazing today." He leaned down and pressed his lips to her forehead. "I'll rub your back for you, after dinner."

She shrugged. "You don't have to do that." Though the thought of him rubbing her back and a lot of other places sent shivers of excitement throughout her body. That little bit of anticipation chased away some of the ache in her back.

"I know I don't have to." He touched his lips to her temple. "But I'd like to."

Lily closed her eyes and sighed. "Mmm. Sounds nice." Then she remembered her resolve to leave as soon as the hay was put up. Unfortunately, or maybe fortunately, the rain had delayed her departure even more. Now she'd have to wait for as long as it took for the grass to dry enough to mow. Then they'd cut, rake and bale the round bales.

Then she'd be on her way. To what, she had no idea. For sure, she'd get out of Whiskey Gulch now that Trace was back. If he chose to stay, he needed to marry someone much better than Lily Davidson.

A hard knot formed in her belly. She couldn't stick around and watch another woman give Trace the family he deserved.

As much as she loved when he kissed her, she couldn't stay and be disappointed all over again. Trace hadn't come after her in eleven years. What happened last night had been a fling. She was convenient and willing. Lily refused to be a distraction. She wanted more out of life than Trace could give. She deserved someone who loved her so much he'd move heaven and earth for her. He'd come after her and woo her. Life was too short to settle for scraps. She wanted the whole meal.

Lily stepped backward and out of Trace's arms.

He frowned as his hands dropped to his sides. "What's wrong?"

"I'm starving and can't go downstairs dressed like this." She gave him a weak smile, ducked around him and dived through the door of the room she'd shared with him the night before.

"Lily," Trace called out.

She didn't stop to see what he wanted. Instead, she closed the door and leaned against it. Her heart wanted her to open the door. Her head made her pull her hand away from the knob. "I can't do this to myself," she whispered. "I can't keep loving him."

After she'd dressed in jeans and a soft white blouse, she took her time brushing the tangles out of her hair. Purposely procrastinating, hoping he'd eat and go to bed, she finally gave in to her rumbling belly. She had to eat. After burning so many calories hauling hay, she needed to refuel her body.

Easing the door open, she looked out into the hallway. Bumping into Trace again would ruin her efforts to get her head on straight. The man sent her thoughts whirling. She had to keep it together for the next few days until she could pack up and leave.

The hallway was empty.

Lily sighed and eased out of her bedroom and down the stairs. She tiptoed past the study and entered the kitchen on silent feet.

Rosalynn turned from the stove, holding a mug with

a tea bag string hanging over the side. "Lily, honey, I was just about to make you a tray of food and bring it up."

"That's not necessary," Lily said quietly, glancing over her shoulder, not wanting to run into Trace. Not when her emotions were so overwrought. She wasn't sure how she'd keep from falling into his arms when that was all she wanted to do.

"If you're looking for Trace, he went out to the barn with Irish to check on the animals and that darn cat." Rosalynn set her mug on the counter. "Sit. I'll serve up a bowl of the stew I made for dinner."

"Thank you," Lily said. "But I can help myself."

"Don't be silly. You're bound to be exhausted."

"As are you," Lily protested.

"I didn't do as much as you."

"You did every bit as much."

"Sit." Rosalynn pointed to the kitchen table. In her "mom" voice, she said, "I insist."

Lily grinned. "Yes, ma'am." She pulled out a chair and sat, releasing a sigh. "It really does feel good to sit."

"Uh-huh." Rosalynn scooped a ladle full of steaming stew into a bowl, grabbed a spoon from a drawer and crossed the kitchen to set them in front of Lily. "Tea?"

"Please." Lily inhaled the hearty aroma of stew and nearly fell into it. She was so tired. "I'm hungry, but I don't know if I'll stay awake to eat this." She drew in another breath and closed her eyes. "It smells so good." She dug the spoon in and carried a heaping helping of beef, carrots and potatoes to her mouth.

Rosalynn brought over another mug of tea along with her own and sat across the table from Lily. "Eat before you sleep. You worked hard today."

Lily nodded and consumed half of the bowl of stew before she paused.

Rosalynn smiled. "Feel better?"

"I do." Lily removed the tea bag from the mug, stirred in a spoonful of sugar and sipped the steaming brew. "This is perfect."

"Speaking of perfect…" Rosalynn set her mug on the table. "When are you and Trace going to stop dancing around and realize you two are perfect for each other?"

As if hit by a strong wind, all of Lily's thoughts of sleep flew out the window. "Excuse me?"

"You heard me. I know you love him. Why don't you tell him?" Rosalynn stared across the table at Lily, an eyebrow cocked in challenge.

Lily gulped. "I can't."

"Can't or won't?" Rosalynn sighed and looked down at her mug. "Look, it's none of my business what you two do with your lives, but, damn it, I want grandchildren before I die."

Her words stabbed Lily right in the heart.

She wanted children. Trace's children. Nothing would make her happier. "I don't think Trace loves me as much as I love him."

"Are you kidding me?" Rosalynn looked at her as if she'd lost her mind. "He can't take his eyes off you. He dogs your every step. If that's not love, I don't know what is."

"Lust," Lily suggested. "If he really loved me, he wouldn't have stayed away for eleven years."

"He thought you were married to someone else."

"He didn't bother to find out whether or not I had, or to try to change my mind." Lily gave Trace's mother a weak smile. "I deserve someone who loves me enough to fight for me. A man who won't take *bug off* for an answer."

"You want to marry a stalker." Rosalynn frowned. "You turned Trace away with a lie. You broke his heart. Why not set the record straight and see where you go from there? What's it going to hurt?"

The food in Lily's belly churned. "What if…?"

"If you don't own up to your lie, how will you ever know what he wants?" Rosalynn reached across the table for Lily's hand. "Lily, I don't want to see you two suffer. And I want—"

"Grandchildren." Lily squeezed Mrs. Travis's hand. "I know."

Rosalynn shook her head. "Yes, I want grandchildren, but more than that, I want to see my child happy. He hasn't been happy for the past eleven years." She laughed, the sound less than humorous. "Believe me, a mother knows." Her smile faded. "And you've come to be like the daughter I never had. I want you to be happy, too. I love you, Lily. I don't want you and Trace to waste another day apart if you were meant to be together."

Tears welled in Lily's eyes. "What if we're not meant to be together?" She swallowed hard.

The clump of boots on the porch heralded the return of Trace and Irish from the barn.

Lily brushed tears from her cheeks. "I have to go."

Rosalynn retained her hold on her hand. "Think about it, will ya?"

With a nod, Lily pulled her hand free and raced out of the kitchen, up the stairs and into her bedroom. Once inside, she closed the door, then leaned her back against the panel and slid to the floor, tears coursing down her cheeks.

Lily had loved Trace for what felt like all of her life. She couldn't bear it if she told him she loved him and he didn't love her in return.

TRACE HELD THE door for Irish and followed him into the kitchen. Everything was as it should have been in the barn. No one had jumped out to hurt them. The buddy system seemed to be working.

His mother sat at the table, staring toward the opposite door leading into the rest of the house.

"Everything all right?" Trace asked.

She glanced at him. "You tell me." His mother pushed to her feet. "Your father is dead, someone is attacking the people who live and work on this ranch, and you're an idiot." She stalked out of the kitchen.

Trace followed her into the living room, where she took down the photo on the fireplace mantel of her wedding day almost forty years ago. "Why did you have to leave me?" she cried, tears rolling down her cheeks as she sank onto the sofa, hugging the framed photo to her chest.

Trace sat next to his mother and slipped an arm around her shoulders.

She turned and buried her face against his shirt. For a long moment, she let the tears fall.

His heart aching, Trace held his mother, knowing how much she'd relied on his father to be there, protect her and run the ranch. Now she was on her own and dealing with a much more difficult situation. He plucked a tissue from the box on the end table and handed it to her.

His mother wiped her eyes and blew her nose before she finally said, "I'm sorry I called you an idiot."

"I'm sure you have every right to call me that. I've been an idiot for more than ten years," he offered.

"Yes, you have," she agreed.

His chest tightened. "I should have cleared the air with Dad a long time ago. I hate to think he died believing I didn't love him."

His mother frowned. "He knew. He felt the same. But that wasn't why I was calling you an idiot."

Trace narrowed his eyes and stared down at his mother. "No? Then what else have I been an idiot about?"

She shook her head. "You have regrets that you didn't patch things up with your father before he died, but you're not looking at what you could do while you still can."

"I can't change things between me and Dad."

His mother smiled. "No, but you can change things between you and people who are still among the living."

His eyes narrowed. "Do I need to fix things between me and you?"

His mother rolled her eyes and sighed. "Of course not. You can be just as hardheaded and dense as your father. When it comes to the women in your life, you really don't have a clue." She set the photo on the coffee table, pushed to her feet and turned to face him. "You love her. It's as clear as the nose on your face. Why don't you tell her, before you lose her?"

"Oh… We're not talking about you and Dad." Trace couldn't try to pretend he didn't know who his mother was talking about. "That's complicated."

"Sweetheart, it's a lot less complicated than you think." She touched his shoulder. "I love you, Trace.

I don't want you to lose this chance to be happy." Her jaw firmed. "Don't screw this up. Now, I'm going to bed." With that, she left the living room and climbed the stairs.

Trace stared at the photograph of his mother and father and wished he could have a marriage like theirs. They'd been together for almost forty years, fighting, bickering and loving each other all that time. Yet they always overcame their differences and never went to bed mad.

Trace's heart tugged hard. His mother had lost not only her husband, but also her best friend.

When Lily had told Trace she was going to marry Matt, Trace had lost the woman he'd loved and his best friend. Dating after Lily had been a useless effort. Once burned, he'd been twice shy, unwilling to risk his heart again, only to have some woman wreck his emotions the way Lily had. He'd been so devastated, it had taken him years and a number of dangerous deployments to harden his heart and get over her.

Only seeing her again had brought back everything he'd thought he'd overcome. He couldn't deny how he felt. His chest hurt and his gut clenched every time he thought of her with someone else.

Hell, he still loved her.

His mother was right. He needed to tell her how he felt and ask her if she felt the same. The sooner he did that, the better off he'd be. If she didn't return his feelings, she'd tell him. Then he could get on with his life.

With this plan in mind, he headed for her bedroom, taking the stairs to the upper landing two at a time. Now that he was ready to move forward, he wanted to get it over with, rip the bandage off and see if the wound had healed.

He hurried past the door to his room and paused in front of Lily's. Raising his hand to knock, he froze.

For a man who'd charged into battle and stared death in the eye, Trace was suddenly more afraid than he'd ever been.

He closed his eyes, sucked in a deep breath and let it out slowly. He wouldn't know until he asked. Forcing his hand to move, he tapped softly on the door and waited.

A moment passed…then two…

"Lily?" he called out softly.

Another few seconds later and no response came from inside her room.

Trace's hand dropped to the doorknob and he twisted it.

The door opened.

He poked his head inside and whispered, "Lily?"

The lights were off. A shadowy lump in the bed didn't move.

Crossing the room, Trace came to a halt beside her bed and stared down at her in the starlight streaming through the window beside her, glinting off her hair, turning it a gray blue in the night.

She lay curled on her side, a hand tucked beneath her cheek, her breathing deep and steady.

The woman was sound asleep. After hauling hay and helping dress a hog, she had to be beyond exhausted.

Now that he'd decided to open up about his feelings, Trace wanted to shake her awake and tell her. But he couldn't bring himself to wake her. She needed to sleep, to recharge her tired body.

Bending over her, he pressed a featherlight kiss to her forehead. "I love you, Lily Davidson," he whispered. "I always have."

Her brow puckered slightly, but she didn't open her eyes and respond.

Disappointed that he'd have to wait and say it again, Trace straightened and backed out of the room, pausing at the door to look at her one more time. Finally, he pulled the door closed and descended the stairs, too wound up to sleep.

He entered his father's study and sat behind the desk.

They'd been so worried about getting the hay cut and stored, he hadn't thought about the business side of running the ranch. Not that he felt like looking at accounts, but someone had to get a handle on things. His father had always been the one to handle the books.

Unopened mail littered his father's desktop. Trace glanced at the senders and sorted the envelopes into a pile for bills and another for miscellaneous. He'd go through them tomorrow.

One by one, he opened the drawers. In the top right-hand drawer, he found several envelopes addressed to his APO location when he'd been deployed to Afghanistan. His last assignment before coming home for his father's funeral.

Curious, he turned over the first one. It hadn't been sealed, nor did it have a stamp on the front.

Trace pulled out a letter, folded neatly into thirds.

When he unfolded it, his father's bold handwriting filled the paper in thick strokes.

The first words at the top captured his attention and made him drop back in his father's chair.

Dear Trace,

I should have written you as soon as you left to join the army. I should have sent letters while you were going through basic combat training. I should have been there for your graduation. Arrogance has a way of making you a lesser person without even trying. I wish I could take back all the wasted years and start over in my relationship with you.

I'd start with telling you a few truths.

I was wrong.

I should never have assumed that just because you were my son, that you'd stay and work the ranch and love it as much as I have. Whiskey Gulch Ranch was my grandfather's dream, my father's life and now mine. It didn't have to be yours. I know that now. You have every right to follow your own path.

Sadly, I can't change the past. But I hope that you can forgive this old man for some of the harsh things he said.

I was wrong.

You are a smart, motivated, hardworking man. No matter the career you choose to pursue, you will succeed.

I was wrong about your sweetheart, Lily. She is not the product of her lineage. Or perhaps she is. Because of who her parents are, she's become a strong, independent and caring young woman. I know now I would have been proud to welcome her into our family as your wife. I wish I hadn't been so pigheaded and obstinate when you first showed interest in her. I hope someday to make it up to her, and to you, for ruining things between the two of you.

Above all, I want you to know how very proud I am of all you have accomplished in the army. I can only hope to understand the training, dedication and commitment it takes to live the life of a Delta Force soldier.

Son, I love you and want you to live the life you choose. If that's remaining in Delta Force, I am at peace with it. You should not be saddled with the responsibility of this ranch. If you choose someday to return and run Whiskey Gulch Ranch, you know I will be happy. But only if you are.

Well, enough of my rambling. I wish you good health and happiness from the bottom of my heart. All my love,
Dad

Trace's heart squeezed so hard in his chest, he thought it might explode. His eyes stung and the hand holding the letter shook.

All the years of anger and disappointment fell away in that one letter.

In that moment, Trace wished he could have had one more conversation with his father. One more chance to mend the fences, to make things right between them. His father had redeemed his side through his letter. But he'd died not knowing that Trace had forgiven him and loved him.

Regret ate a hole in his gut and reminded him that he couldn't waste a single moment wallowing in the past. He had to live in the present and ensure the future wasn't lost as well. He had to make it right with Lily before he could get on with his life. He prayed he had time. Living to the next day wasn't guaranteed.

His father had proved that.

Chapter Fifteen

Lily woke early the next morning with a headache like nobody's business. Quietly, she dressed, grabbed her boots, and tiptoed out of her room and down the stairs, well before the sun rose in the eastern sky.

She hoped to get outside and take care of the animals before anyone else got out of bed.

Sounds from the kitchen made her turn in that direction.

Rosalynn stood at the stove, laying strips of bacon into a frying pan.

"You're up extra early." Lily sat in one of the chairs at the kitchen table and slid her right foot into a boot.

Rosalynn looked over her shoulder with a weak smile. "Couldn't sleep. The bed is so big and empty."

Lily's chest tightened. "I'm so sorry." She shoved her left foot into the opposite boot and pushed to her feet. "Is there anything I can do to help?"

Rosalynn snorted. "Since you can't bring James back, I assume you're talking about cooking." She tipped her head toward the refrigerator. "You could get the eggs and butter out."

"I can do that. Just don't ask me to make the eggs over easy, unless you like them lacy and burned." She reached into the fridge and extracted a carton of eggs and a tub of butter. "My mother wasn't much of a cook. I must have gotten my lack of skills from her."

"You're much more comfortable working outside with the animals," Rosalynn said without any kind of judgment. She flipped a piece of bacon over in the pan. "What's your plan for the day?"

"I have a few errands to run in town. Hopefully, by later this afternoon, the fields will be dry enough to cut." In town, she planned to run by the bank, withdraw her savings and close her account, the first task in her plan. Once the last of the hay was cut and properly stored, she would leave Whiskey Gulch Ranch and her hometown. Staying would only cause her more heartache. She loved Trace. If he didn't love her as much as she loved him, she needed to move on.

Her heart heavy, Lily slid bread into the toaster and waited while it cooked.

Rosalynn broke a dozen eggs into a bowl, whipped them with a wire whisk until they were fluffy and poured them into the skillet. Then she turned to Lily. "What's wrong?"

Lily's head jerked up. "Wrong? What do you mean?"

"You've been frowning since you walked through that door."

Guilt rode up her cheeks in a wave of heat. "I'm sorry. I didn't realize I was frowning." Lily concentrated on easing the tension out of her face. "Is that better?" she asked.

Rosalynn shook her head. "It's not the frown that was bothering me. It's the fact that you're frowning. I think of you as the daughter I never had. When you're stressed, I'm stressed. When you're unhappy, I'm unhappy."

Lily abandoned her duties at the toaster and crossed to the older woman, pulling her into a hug. "I don't want you to be any unhappier than you already are because of me."

"Then tell me what's wrong and let me see if I can help make it right." Rosalynn set her at arm's length. "So?"

Lily laughed, though it took effort. She'd miss this woman who'd given her a job and made her a part of her family. "You can't fix everything."

"I might if I know what the problem is." She cocked an eyebrow. "Does it have to do with my pigheaded son?" She shook her head. "He takes after his father more than he can ever imagine."

Lily laughed for real this time. "I see it." She smiled at Rosalynn. "You're an amazing woman, you know that?"

Mrs. Travis's brows dipped. "I don't think so. I'm just someone who's trying to get through the day."

"That's what I mean." Lily took her hand and stared at her long fingers, the calluses, cuts and nicks marring the skin. "You just lost your husband, yet you're worried about others' happiness."

Rosalynn shrugged. "I need to be needed and to keep busy. If I sit around with nothing to do, or no one to worry about, I have too much time to ruminate about my own problems." She gave Lily a sad smile. "So, if I can help you, I'd love the opportunity."

Lily hugged her, hating the idea of leaving this woman who'd become more of a mother to her than her own. "I love you, Rosalynn Travis. No matter what, remember that."

After a moment, Rosalynn leaned back. "You say that like you're going somewhere."

"I am," Lily said. "I'm going to town to run some errands after I take care of the animals."

"If your problems include my son," Rosalynn started, "just know, he's a man. And some men aren't good at expressing their feelings. Take James, for example… he rarely told me that he loved me."

"Really?" Lily leaned back. "Everyone could tell you hung the moon in his eyes."

The older woman nodded. "Yes, but he didn't say it. Instead, he lived it. Every time he held the door for me, brought me wildflowers from the fields, held my hand when he walked with me and never started eating before I sat at the dinner table. He didn't have to tell me. I knew he loved me by the little things he did.

"Trace is so much like his father, sometimes it scares me. At others, it makes me happy. I can see James in his face and demeanor. My husband isn't completely gone. He lives on in my son and in my heart."

Tears welled in Lily's eyes. "Yes, he does resemble his father." Rosalynn and James Travis had lived the life Lily had always dreamed of. Not the rich rancher life, but the life of a couple who continued to love each other through thick and thin.

"Tell you what, I don't like the idea of you going to town on your own. Want me to ask one of the guys to go with you?" Rosalynn asked.

Lily held up her hands. "No, that's okay. I can manage on my own."

"With all that's been happening lately, I don't feel

comfortable having any one of us going off alone. Irish headed out to the barnyard a few minutes before you came downstairs. Help him find his way around while I cook. When I have breakfast ready, I'll go with you to town. I could do a little grocery shopping while you run your errands."

Lily hesitated for a split second. She didn't want anyone knowing her plan to leave. Until she drove away from Whiskey Gulch Ranch, she wouldn't tell anyone that she didn't plan to return. But if Rosalynn wanted to grocery shop, she could do that while Lily headed to the bank across the street to close her account. "Sounds like a good plan. I'll be back as soon as the animals are fed and watered."

Lily left the house and headed for the barn. She'd really wanted to leave for town before Trace woke. But that wasn't an option, unless she wanted to wait in her SUV until the bank opened at nine o'clock.

Waiting patiently was never one of Lily's strengths. She'd be better off mucking stalls and currying the entire stable full of horses until their coats shone. At least her hands and mind would be too busy to dwell on her impending departure from the ranch.

She found Irish in the barn, bent low, petting Patches.

"You're up early," he said, straightening.

"Couldn't sleep. Thought I'd get an early start cleaning stalls."

"I'm still new to this ranching gig, but I'm willing to learn and working on getting my strength back. Won't be long before I'm tossing eighty-pound bales with the best of them." He winked. "What's on the honey-do list for this morning?"

"You can feed the horses and the chickens. Beware

of the rooster. If he feels the need to defend his hens, use the fishnet hanging on the side of the barn to contain him."

Irish frowned. "Contain?"

Lily laughed. "You scoop him up and hang him on the hook on the barn until you've poured the feed in the chicken pen."

He nodded. "Never knew that was what fishnets were for." He chuckled. "Learn something new every day."

Lily snapped a lead on Lady and led her out of her stall. She tied the lead to a hook and went to work on mucking the stall. When Irish returned from feeding the chickens and the other horses, she had him brush Lady.

Ten wheelbarrows full of sludge from the bottom of the first two stalls and Lily needed a shower before she went to town.

Irish ducked his head into the stall she had just finished. "Mrs. Travis called out that breakfast is ready."

She carried her rake out and hung it on the wall, then followed Irish out of the barn to the house.

He held the door for her to enter first.

Thankfully, Trace wasn't in the kitchen when she passed through. With thoughts of leaving heavy on her mind, she didn't want to run into him, afraid he'd see her face and guess. Or worse, he'd see her and not give a damn.

She made it through the house and into her room without running into him. After grabbing clean clothing, she poked her head out the door. The hallway was clear. Lily ran across to the bathroom and locked herself inside.

She stripped out of her dirty jeans and shirt and hurried through a quick but thorough shower, washing the manure, straw and sweat from her body. When she finished, she dried, dressed and ran a brush through her wet hair. She didn't want to take the time to apply a blow dryer to the wet strands. The hot Texas sun would dry it soon enough.

Squaring her shoulders, she opened the bathroom door and stepped out into the hallway. If she ran into Trace, she told herself that she could handle it.

"I can," she whispered, knowing she might melt into a puddle of goo if he looked at her just right. Eleven years had passed, and she'd never gotten over the man.

Voices rose from the floor below.

Lily's heartbeat sputtered and then raced. She gripped the rail as she descended the stairs to the ground floor.

Rosalynn stood in the foyer with Trace, Irish and Roy. She grimaced when she spotted Lily. "Lily, honey, I won't be able to go with you to town after all." Turning, she waved a hand toward her son. "Trace has graciously offered to accompany you, if that's okay."

No, it wasn't okay. Lily's heart sank into her kneecaps. The last thing she needed was to be cooped up in the same vehicle with Trace, especially when she was going to clear her bank account. He might get nosy and ask why. Then she'd have to lie or tell him the truth. Either way…she didn't want to know how he'd feel.

Lily stiffened her back. What he thought or didn't think about her didn't matter. She deserved someone who would fight for her. Someone who loved her enough to tell her.

Trace wasn't that guy. He'd stepped away from her without an attempt to change her mind. He'd left Whiskey Gulch and had remained gone for over ten years. Why would he care about her?

"Fine," Lily said. "But I hope you have things to do, because I don't want you hanging around while I conduct my business."

Trace popped a sharp salute in her direction. "Yes, ma'am."

Lily rolled her eyes. "Oh, and you don't have to call me ma'am. It makes me uncomfortable."

"Yes, your highness," he said with a wink. Before she could protest, he turned and addressed his mother. "We'll be back soon. I thought we'd use the rest of the day to check the fences."

"Sounds like a good plan," his mother said. "The fields should be dry enough tomorrow to mow."

"That's what we're banking on." He leaned down and kissed his mother's cheek. Then he glanced at Irish.

Irish nodded. "I've got her covered."

"Thank you."

"Aren't you going to have breakfast first?" Rosalynn asked.

Lily shook her head. "Thanks, but I'm not hungry."

"In that case—" Trace opened the front door and peered out before moving to the side with a flourish of his arm "—your chariot awaits."

Lily rolled her eyes and marched through the door and out to Trace's truck. She stayed a step ahead of him, hurrying so that she would open her own door.

Frustratingly, he kept up and reached around her to open her door, his arm brushing across hers.

A shiver of awareness rippled through her, throwing her off guard. Damn. Damn. Damn. This little trip to town was going to be harder than she expected.

Once they were both inside, buckled and on their way, Trace turned to her. "What's wrong?"

Lily snapped, "Why does everyone assume something's wrong?"

He blinked and snorted. "It was a simple question. If everything was all right in your world, you would have answered without jumping down my throat."

"I'm not jumping down your throat," she said, toning down her argument, realizing she was overreacting to his question. Folding her hands in her lap, she drew in a deep, calming breath and let it out. "Nothing's wrong."

"Then why are you avoiding me?" he asked.

Heat filled her cheeks and her fingers curled into the denim on her legs. "I'm not avoiding you," she lied.

"Lily, you never were a good liar." He glanced at her hands in her lap. "Your face is red, and your hands are clenching."

Lily straightened her hands on her thighs and willed the heat out of her face. "I'm fine. And I don't want to talk."

"Okay." He drove for another minute without saying a word. The minute stretched into two very long minutes before he broke the silence. "While you're doing your thing, I thought I'd stop by the sheriff's office and see if they've had any leads on my father's murder."

A frown pulled Lily's brow low. "I'd like to be there when you talk to the sheriff."

"Okay." Trace nodded. "I can wait for you."

"Thank you."

"Where do you want to go first?" he asked.

"The bank," she said. "I'm low on cash. I need to make a withdrawal."

"Drive-through?"

Lily shook her head. "I'd prefer to go inside."

Trace drove into town and parked in the bank parking lot.

"I'll only be a short time," Lily said.

He'd started to unbuckle his belt but paused. "I'll wait here."

Lily hurried out of the vehicle and into the bank. She skipped the teller and went to one of the account managers. "I'd like to close my account and withdraw all my money."

Cecilia Menn was someone Lily had gone to high school with. She frowned. "Is everything okay, Lily?"

Lily's eyes stung, but she managed a nod. "Everything's fine. I'm just moving."

"I'm sorry to hear that," Cecilia said as she typed on her keyboard. "Don't you want to leave the account open until you're established in your new home and then transfer the money over?"

Lily shook her head. "No, I want to withdraw all of it and close it. I'm not sure how long it will take me to find a new bank." A new job and a place to live. Hell, she had no idea where she was going. Just away from Whiskey Gulch. Maybe she'd go to San Antonio. She'd always wanted to visit the Alamo. Her chest tightened. This town had been her life. Not always a good life, but it had been her home since the day she was born. Leaving was going to be harder than she thought. Especially because she was leaving behind the only man she'd ever loved. Tears welled in her eyes.

Cecilia reached across the desk. "Are you okay?" She plucked a tissue from the box on the corner of her desk and handed it to Lily.

"I'm fine. Just a little nostalgic." Lily pressed the

tissue to the corners of her eyes, refusing to let the tears slip down her cheeks. Trace couldn't know that she was crying. She never cried in front of him. She wouldn't start now.

"Do you want all cash, a check or a mix?" Cecilia asked.

"Cash."

"That's a lot of cash to carry around," Cecilia warned.

Not really, Lily thought. Not considering it was her life savings. She just hoped she didn't have to use it all before she found another job, in another town. Not to mention an apartment, deposits on an apartment, utilities and more. She might last a couple months before she ran out of funds.

She carried a cashier's check to the teller, who counted out the sum of her savings in hundreds and some change. Lily stuffed the wad of bills into her purse and zipped the opening, feeling like a bank robber making a run for it.

Cecilia closed her account and came around her desk to give her a hug. "I wish you well. And know that you'll be missed in Whiskey Gulch."

"I doubt that," she murmured.

Cecilia caught her arms and stared into her eyes. "I'll miss you. You've always been kind to me when others haven't been."

"Thank you, Cecelia, and likewise. I will miss you." Lily hugged the account manager and made a dash for the door, praying she didn't burst into tears in front of Trace.

She climbed up into the truck, averting her gaze. When Trace didn't move to start the engine, Lily forced herself to look through the windshield at the street leading to the sheriff's office. "Think they will have found any more information?" Out of the corner of her eye, she could see Trace staring at her.

"We can hope," Trace said. Finally, he started the engine and drove out of the parking lot and down Main Street to the sheriff's office.

When he parked, he remained in his seat a moment longer than necessary. "Look, Lily, if I've said anything or done anything to upset you, I wish you'd tell me. I can't read minds."

"Don't worry," she said, grabbing for the door handle. "You haven't done anything. I told you, I'm fine." Lily pushed open the door and slid down from her seat.

Trace joined her at the front of the truck. He hooked her elbow in his hand and guided her into the office.

Sheriff Owens met them with an outstretched hand. "I'm glad you came by. I had a visit from Marty Bains this morning."

"Why did he come in?" Lily asked.

"I told him and Alan that if they remembered anything about that day of James Travis's murder, no matter how insignificant it might be, to bring it to me."

"And?" Trace prompted.

"He said he remembered looking for the four-wheelers in an outbuilding. He found one, but the other was missing." The sheriff frowned. "He was going to ask Mr. Travis about it, but that's about the time Mr. Travis's horse brought him home."

"Why did he think that was important?" Trace asked.

The sheriff's jaw tightened. "He said it was there that morning."

"If he was working around the barn all day, wouldn't he have heard it moved?" Lily asked.

"He said the only time he and Alan weren't near the outbuildings was at lunch," Sheriff Owens said. "Mrs. Travis invited them in for sandwiches."

"What about Roy? Where was he?" Trace asked.

The sheriff nodded. "I asked the same question. Marty said Roy left the ranch earlier that day, claiming he had errands to run in town."

"So, no one saw who took the four-wheeler," Trace said. "And that four-wheeler is still missing. It could be the person who stole the four-wheeler was the same one shooting at us when we were cutting hay two days ago."

Lily's fists bunched. Trace had nearly been shot that day. It was also the day he'd gotten into an altercation with Matt.

"If we could find that four-wheeler, we might lift some latent prints," the sheriff said.

"A big if." Lily sighed. "We'll keep our eyes open for it. Thanks for letting us know."

"One other thing," Sheriff Owens said. "The medical examiner said the bullet that killed your father was fired in an upward trajectory. Since your father was riding a horse, the shooter had to have been on the ground and close by. If we could find the location of the crime, we might find the bullet casings nearby. It wasn't like the shooter was a sniper several hundred yards away." The sheriff's lips pressed into a firm line. "That's if we can find the crime scene."

"When it could have happened anywhere on the twelve hundred acres of Whiskey Gulch Ranch..." Trace started.

"And it's rained since then…" Lily added.

"It's highly unlikely we'll find the exact spot," the sheriff concluded. "But it's good to know, in case we do."

As they left the sheriff's office, a large, black SUV pulled up next to Trace's pickup and Oswald Young leaned out the window. "Trace, you got a minute?"

Trace crossed to where the other man sat in his vehicle. "What's up?"

"One of my guides was out setting up hunting stands today and noticed some cattle ranging on the Rocking J Ranch."

"So?" Trace asked.

"We aren't running cattle on the Rocking J Ranch. We're a game outfitting ranch. We sold off all but a few head of cattle and keep them in a pasture close to the lodge. My foreman checked and the cattle he found are branded with WG."

"The Whiskey Gulch brand," Trace concluded. "We must have a fence down. If we come collect the cattle, will you have hunters out there shooting at us?"

Oswald shook his head. "We're holding off all hunting until the cattle have been rounded up and removed from the premises."

"So, the sooner we get them off, the sooner your hunters can get back to what they pay you for." Trace held out his hand. "On our way now."

"Thank you. Let me know if you need help. My guys aren't cowboys, but they can lend a hand if needed."

"I think we can handle getting the cattle back over on the Whiskey Gulch and fix the break in the fence," Trace said.

"Thanks." Oswald tipped his head toward the sheriff's office. "Did they find the man who shot your father?"

Trace shook his head. "Not yet."

"I hope they do," Oswald said, a frown creasing his brow. "The sooner, the better. I hate to think there's a killer out there. As an outfitter, it's my responsibility to keep my clients safe."

"That's hard to do when we don't know who killed Mr. Travis," Lily said quietly.

"Exactly." Oswald gave a nod. "Let me know if we can help with rounding up cattle or mending fences. I understand you're shorthanded on the Whiskey Gulch Ranch. But now that you're back, hopefully things will get straightened out."

Lily didn't add that Trace wasn't back for good. Whether he stayed or returned to active duty, she wouldn't know. She'd be somewhere else, starting over and moving on. Lily climbed into the passenger seat of Trace's truck and stared straight ahead.

Trace started around the front of the truck, hesitated and glanced toward Matt's auto shop two blocks away. Then he slipped behind the wheel and drove to the shop, parking out front.

Matt came out, wiping his hands on an oily rag. He tipped his head toward Lily, his gaze turning to Trace. "Everything all right?"

Trace leaned out the window. "If you want to be part of this ranch," he started, "we could use your help rounding up Whiskey Gulch cattle on Rocking J land."

Matt's brow furrowed. "I don't know much about herding cattle, but I'm willing to learn. I'll be out there as soon as I close up the shop."

Trace pulled out of the parking lot onto Main Street, his lips quirking upward. "I wonder if he's ever been on a horse," he muttered.

Lily wondered if Trace was about to test his half brother. "If he hasn't, you might cut him some slack."

Trace's eyes narrowed as he looked across the console at Lily. "He'll have to go on horseback if he's going at all. We don't have four-wheelers to get us there and we don't know if we can get a truck across the terrain. It's hilly and rocky in a lot of areas on the Rocking J."

"I know. Just don't do anything that will get him hurt. After all, you're brothers." She raised an eyebrow and shot a direct glance his way.

"*Half* brothers," Trace corrected.

"No matter how you feel about Matt, you can't give your mother another body to bury," she said, her voice hard, her lips pressed into a thin line. "Matt didn't do anything to you. If you're mad about what happened eleven years ago, blame me."

Trace's hands tightened on the steering wheel until his knuckles turned white. He had driven five miles out of town before he relaxed. He loosened his grip and his fingers turned back to their normal color. "You're right," he said. "My mother doesn't need another body to bury."

A couple of miles passed in a whir of images blurred by unshed tears.

"Why did you lie to me?" Trace asked.

Lily had dreaded that question for the past eleven years. At the same time, she welcomed it. Finally, she could set herself free of the lie. Then she could move on with her life, away from Whiskey Gulch. "You needed to leave."

"I was leaving."

"You were heading into the military. A relationship with me would have dragged you down. Maybe even kept you from getting security clearance. I couldn't let that happen." She drew in a deep breath. "So, I broke up with you in the only way I knew that would keep you from giving up on your decision to join the army."

Trace's foot left the accelerator, the truck slowing almost to a stop on the highway. "That's it? You lied to me about marrying Hennessey so that my clearance would go through?" He shook his head. "That's about the saddest excuse I've ever heard."

"Yeah, well, we were kids. What did you expect? You needed to be free and I needed to grow up and realize what we had would never have lasted." Lily swallowed hard on the sob rising up her throat. "We were from completely different worlds."

"And you didn't give me the opportunity to decide what was good or bad for me. You made up my mind for me." He snorted. "That's a hell of a note." His foot jammed down on the accelerator. "I guess I should say thanks for saving me from a fate worse than death."

The anger in his voice cut through her like a knife. She fought back the tears by urging her own anger to the surface. "You thought everything would be all roses and sunshine. You've never lost a fight just because of who you were associated with. How would you have felt if the army denied your clearance because you were dating a woman whose father was a convicted felon?" She glared at him. "You would have been stuck here in Whiskey Gulch, hating your father and hating me. That's why I lied to you." Tears slipped from her eyes and spilled down her cheeks. "It broke my heart, but I did it for you, damn it."

Trace slowed the truck again, pulled onto the shoulder of the road and shifted into Park.

"What…what are you doing?" Lily blinked back the tears.

"I'm stopping the truck so I can do this." He reached across the seat, unbuckled her seatbelt, gripped her arms, and dragged her over the console and into his lap. Then his lips were crushing hers in a kiss that stole her breath away.

For only a second, she considered fighting him off. Her body and mouth betrayed her. As if of their own accord, her arms snaked around his neck and pressed him closer. When his tongue traced the seam of her lips, she opened to him, meeting him thrust for thrust, loving the way he tasted and felt. He didn't stop kissing her until they were both out of breath and forced to come up for air.

Trace leaned his forehead against hers. "Do you think I cared about what the army decided was good or bad? I would have walked away from the military if they refused to accept me with you."

"Then what? You and your father were butting heads. He didn't like me. I wasn't good enough for his son."

"You were the best thing that ever happened to me, and still are," he said, kissing the tip of her nose.

"What about your military career? Won't they frown on your association with the daughter of a felon?"

He snorted. "If they do, too bad. They'd have to take me as I am, or I walk."

"But you love the army."

"I love you more." He gathered her close and held

her against him in a tight hug. "I don't ever want to be without you. The last eleven years made me realize how much I love you."

"You had eleven years to forget me," she whispered.

"And did you forget me?" he asked, staring down into her eyes.

"I tried," she said. Lily shook her head. "I failed. You were my first...and only love."

Chapter Sixteen

Trace couldn't believe she'd just admitted to loving him. All these years, he'd longed to be right where he was, but he thought he'd lost his chance all those years ago. "I should have come back and fought for you."

"You were busy fighting wars," she said. "But, yes, you should have come back and fought for me, too."

"Can you forgive me for failing as a knight in shining armor?"

"Maybe," she said. "If you can forgive me for the lie I told you about Matt." She bit down on her lip, praying he could.

"I get it now. I didn't get it when I was eighteen." He kissed her again, all the world fading away when his lips touched hers.

The whine of an engine nearing them brought him back to the present and the fact they were parked on the side of the highway, making out.

A motorcycle pulled up beside the truck and stopped.

Trace glanced at the rider as he pulled off his helmet.

Matt Hennessey peered into the truck, his eyes narrowing. "You two all right?"

Trace grinned. "Better than all right."

"Good. I thought you might have broken down." His brow crinkled. "You all right, Lily?"

Lily smiled. "I am."

"Then I'll leave you two to whatever it is you're doing." He slipped the helmet over his head and buckled the strap beneath his chin. "I'll be waiting when you get to the ranch." He glanced at the sun that had slipped past its zenith and was heading toward the horizon. "Don't take too long. No telling how long we'll need to round up those cows." With those parting words, he revved his engine and sped off, kicking up gravel behind him.

Trace sighed. "As much as I'd rather hold you forever, we have cattle to round up."

Lily cupped his cheek and brushed her lips across his. Then she moved back over the console and buckled her seat belt. "Let's do this. Then we can pick up where we left off."

Trace nodded and shifted into Drive. "We need to talk about where we go from here."

"Are we going somewhere?" Lily raised her eyebrows, a smile playing at the corners of her lips.

"Maybe," he said.

She patted her purse. "I'm ready when you are."

He laughed. "What if I decide to stay here?"

She shot a glance in his direction. "Will you be satisfied being just a rancher? I mean, you've been a soldier for eleven years. I'm sure it's more exciting than worming steers."

"I've been thinking about it, and I might have come up with a way to make Whiskey Gulch Ranch a place where I want to stay."

"I'm all ears. Especially if it means I get to see you more often than once every eleven years."

They pulled into the drive leading up to the ranch house.

"We can talk about it tonight," Trace said. "Right now, I need to go find some bovine escapees."

Matt stood beside his motorcycle in the barnyard next to Irish, Trace's mother and Roy.

Feeling lighter and happier than he had in a very long time, Trace climbed out of the truck and hurried around to open the door for Lily. She already had it open, but she waited for him to grip her around the waist and lift her to the ground.

It felt so good to hold her in his hands, Trace didn't want to let go. Alas, others were waiting for him to help.

His mother smiled as he approached them holding Lily's hand. "You two patch things up?"

Trace pulled Lily into the curve of his arm. "I hope so."

Lily laughed and hugged him around the middle. "Me, too."

"If you two think we can get moving, we're burning daylight," Roy said.

"I take it we'll be riding horses out to where the cattle are," Matt said. "I admit, I've only been on a horse maybe a handful of times, many years ago. If you could point me to the horse that knows what to do, maybe he can train me?" He gave a crooked smile.

Lily hurried toward the barn. "I know just the horse. And it's a she, not a he."

Trace nodded. "I believe she means Lady. If you want to help her saddle up, we can get going. Getting the cattle back on this side of the fence won't be hard.

Usually, all we need to do is shake a bucket of grain and they'll come running."

"We'll need to mend the fences," Roy said. "I can drive the tractor out to wherever we find the break."

"I can cover, if you have another horse as tame as Lady," Irish said.

Trace turned to his mother.

She held up her hands. "I'm out this time. Roy took a call from the Meyerses. Seems Chad needs help with Alice. I'm going over to see what I can do for them."

Trace shot a glance toward Irish. "I'd prefer you cover for my mother. We can manage on our own." He turned to Matt. "Are you carrying?"

Matt pulled back his leather jacket, displaying a shoulder holster and a handgun tucked inside. "I'm good to go."

"I've got mine. Plus, I'll bring a rifle, just in case." Trace nodded to Irish. "I want you to go with the women to the Meyerses'."

"Women?" Lily paused as she reached the barn and turned back. "I'm going with you to bring the cattle back."

"Please, go with Mom and Irish," Trace said. "The three of us can keep an eye out for trouble. I'd rather have three of you going to the Meyerses'. Irish is a trained Delta Force soldier. He's good at spotting trouble, and he'll take good care of you."

Irish nodded. "That I will."

Lily's lips pressed into a tight line.

Trace wanted her with him, but he was worried about her being out in the open where a skilled sniper could fire off a round from any direction and take her down. He'd never forgive himself if Lily died because he'd been selfish enough to want her along for the ride. "Please, Lily. My mother might need help with Mrs. Meyers."

Lily held his gaze for a long moment and then nodded. "Okay. But I ride better than Matt, and I know how to fix a fence."

"Matt is also a trained marine," Trace pointed out.

Matt nodded. "I've been deployed four times in five years, fought in battles against enemies we couldn't see. Don't worry," he said. "I'll take care of my half brother."

Lily's face reddened. "Okay. I'll help you saddle up," she said. Then she turned to Trace's mother. "I'll be ready in a few minutes."

His mother nodded.

Lily entered the barn, a frown lowering her brow.

Trace turned to his mother. "We should be back before dark."

"Same here." She touched his arm. "I'm glad you and Lily worked things out."

Trace nodded. "So am I." He bent and pressed a kiss to his mother's cheek. "Thanks for believing in us."

"You only had to believe in each other." She winked. "Now go. You need to get out there and get the cattle back on our spread. I hope to be home in time to rustle up some dinner for you."

"We can fend for ourselves," Trace said.

"Yeah, but I like having my family around me." Her smile faded. "I miss your father."

"I miss him, too."

Roy touched Trace's mother's arm. "Be careful, Ros. You don't know who might be out there. I'd hate to see you hurt."

Trace's mother smiled at Roy. "Thank you, Roy. I'll be careful."

Trace hurried into the barn and saddled Rambo, the black gelding his father had been so proud of. The animal had been trained as a cutting horse. His skills might come in handy if the feed bucket didn't do the trick.

Lily, with Matt's help, finished outfitting Lady with a saddle and bridle and adjusted the stirrups to fit Matt's tall frame.

Within minutes, the horses were ready, and Roy had the tractor out of the shed and waiting on the other side of the gate.

Trace stopped beside Lily and pulled her into his arms for a quick kiss. "Hold that thought until I get back."

"I'll be waiting," she murmured. Lily glanced at the pasture, her brow dipping. "Be careful out there."

He kissed her forehead. "You be careful going over to the Meyerses' place."

Trace mounted his horse and rode through the gate, followed by Matt. His half brother sat his horse well and even posted in his stirrups when Lady broke into a trot.

The man might end up being an asset on the ranch, given time.

Trace glanced back at Lily and his mother, anxious to return and get on with their reunion. He couldn't wait to be with the woman he'd loved for what felt like all of his life.

LILY CLIMBED INTO the driver's seat of Rosalynn's SUV.

Rosalynn slipped into the back seat and Irish into the passenger seat.

The drive over to the Meyerses' place wouldn't have

taken long if they could have driven as the bird flies. But the roads forced them to take the long way around.

Twenty minutes later, they drove up to the older ranch house with the faded paint and a front porch that clearly needed to be leveled and the rotten boards replaced.

The Meyerses hadn't been fortunate enough to have children of their own. They ran cattle on their place, but not many. Because of hospital bills and the seven-year drought, they had sold two-thirds of their herd several years ago and were living on what was left of the proceeds.

Chad Meyers stepped out onto the porch, shading his eyes as the SUV pulled up to the house.

Rosalynn, Irish and Lily got out of the vehicle and approached the man.

"This is a nice surprise," Mr. Meyers said. He pushed a hand through his shock of white hair that appeared as if he hadn't combed it in several days. "To what do I owe the pleasure?"

Rosalynn frowned. "Roy said you'd called and needed help with Alice. We came over as soon as we could."

Mr. Meyers's fuzzy white brows dipped. "I didn't call your place." He turned toward the screen door. "Alice?"

An older woman using a walker pushed through the door and out onto the porch. She smiled at them. "You didn't tell me we had guests," she said. "Rosalynn, Lily, it's so good to see you." She turned to Irish. "I don't believe we've met."

Irish climbed the steps. "I'm Joseph Monahan, but folks call me Irish."

"Irish, so nice to meet you. Please, come in." Mrs. Meyers held the door for them. "I just made a pitcher of iced tea."

Rosalynn climbed the porch steps but didn't enter. "It's good to see you up and about." She hugged the woman and stepped back, frowning. "But I don't understand. Roy assured me you'd called and needed help."

Alice Meyers smiled. "So nice of you to come, but I didn't call." She turned to her husband.

"I didn't, either," he said. "The missus has been doing so much better, I thought I might take her to the town for supper tonight."

Rosalynn tapped a finger to her chin. "That's strange. Why would Roy tell me you needed help?"

Chad shook his head. "I don't know. It doesn't make sense. We haven't run into him but at the feed store maybe a handful of times since he went to work for the Whiskey Gulch Ranch."

"Was the same when he worked at the T-Bar M Ranch when he worked for the Talbots," Alice said. "Rarely saw him. He spent most of his time on the ranch."

"Heard he was sweet on Mona Talbot after her husband fell off his horse and died," Alice said.

"He kept the ranch running for several months following Mike's death."

"Then Mona's grown children stepped in and talked her into selling the place. The new owners replaced Roy with their own foreman. Roy was brokenhearted about Mona leaving. He had big plans for the ranch. I think he wanted to marry Mona and take over."

Lily's chest tightened. "I didn't know this."

Alice waved a hand. "It's all gossip we talked about at the monthly quilting bee."

"All I knew was Roy applied for the job. Since he had experience, James hired him," Rosalynn said. She looked up at Alice. "You say Mr. Talbot fell off his horse?"

Chad nodded. "They speculate the horse came across a snake and threw him. He lay for several hours before anyone found him."

"Where was Roy when that happened?" Irish asked.

A sinking feeling hit the pit of Lily's belly.

"Said he was on his way into town for supplies," Alice said. "Why?"

Lily's gaze met Irish's and then moved to Rosalynn's.

"We need to go," Rosalynn said. "Now." She smiled at Alice and Chad. "Let us know if you do need help." She hurried down the steps and half ran toward the SUV.

Lily followed.

"Nice to meet you," Irish said behind her and quickly caught up. "I'll drive."

Lily shook her head. "I'd rather you kept your hands free."

He nodded and held the door for Rosalynn as she slid into the back seat.

Once they were all in the vehicle, Lily drove away from the Meyerses' house. As soon as she was out of sight, she pressed her foot to the accelerator and raced out to the highway.

"How could it be?" Rosalynn sat forward in the back seat, her gaze on the road ahead. "He's always been so nice to me."

"He was nice to Mona Talbot," Lily said.

"Do you really think he expected to marry Mona and take over the ranch?" Rosalynn asked, shaking her head.

"We could be grasping at straws here," Irish said.

"What exactly are we saying?" Lily asked, knowing the answer, but wanting to hear it stated aloud.

"Roy could have been the one to steal the four-wheeler," Irish said.

"He could have been the one to kill James," Rosalynn whispered, her face pale, her fingers turning white on the back of the seat.

"If he thought he could murder your husband—" Irish shot a glance back at Rosalynn "—he might also think he has to do away with your husband's two children in order to get to you."

More color drained from Rosalynn's face.

Lily turned in her seat and covered Trace's mother's hand with hers. "If that's what's happening, the guys are trained combatants. They can defend themselves."

"If they see it coming," Rosalynn argued.

"Besides, there are two of them and one of Roy," Irish pointed out.

"We don't know if any of this speculation is even accurate," Lily said, though deep in her gut, she could feel the truth.

Her gaze on the road ahead, Rosalynn said, "Could you go a little faster?"

"Got the pedal to the floor, ma'am," Lily said, only slowing for curves.

The twenty minutes it took to get to the Whiskey Gulch Ranch felt like hours.

Chapter Seventeen

Trace and Matt rode out on horseback, following the fence line bordering the Rocking J Ranch. Trace carried a sack of feed strapped behind his saddle.

Roy was to follow on the tractor as best he could, depending on the terrain, until they found where the fence was down.

After riding for twenty minutes, Trace noticed the barbed wire was loose on the fence beside him.

"Looks like we're getting to the break in the fence," he said to Matt. He turned to his half brother. "How are you holding up?"

Matt adjusted himself in the saddle. "So far so good. Have to admit, the seat on my motorcycle is a lot softer than this saddle."

Trace nodded. "It takes time to build up calluses. It's been a while since I was horseback riding. I'll be sore as well. This is what it's like to be a rancher." He stared at the man he'd have to share his inheritance with. "Are you up for it?"

Matt shrugged. "I've been in more uncomfortable places."

"Same," Trace said.

"Are you ready to take on the responsibility of running a ranch?" Matt asked.

"I know how," Trace said. "I just didn't figure on coming back to this life so soon."

"Civilian life moves at a much slower pace in some cases," Matt said. "You're used to high-paced action and making a difference in the lives of people who desperately need you." He looked into the distance. "Coming off active duty is an adjustment in itself. The combat skills you trained so hard to perfect aren't as marketable."

"Tell me about it." Trace's lips twisted. "Ranching is in my blood. I learned to ride a horse almost before I learned to walk."

"I didn't grow up on a ranch. But I learn quickly. I didn't ask for your inheritance. I don't want it."

"Yeah, but we're stuck with each other. If you sell, we both sell."

"The question is, do you want the ranch to go out of the family?" Matt asked.

"It's not about me," Trace said. "We're in this together, like it or not."

Matt sighed. "If we don't want to sell Whiskey Gulch Ranch, can we work together to manage the ranch without killing each other or going insane with the slower pace and less fulfilling lifestyle?"

"That's the sixty-four-million-dollar question." Could he work with this interloper? To be fair, Matt hadn't asked to be included in the inheritance. And he hadn't had the privilege of choosing his father. He, like Trace, had the DNA he was born with. By accident of birth, Trace and Matt were related.

It could be worse. Matt wasn't all bad. He'd served

in the marines and worked hard to make a living. He wasn't into drugs and he appeared to be honorable and respectful of women.

Trace glanced ahead. "Here we are. This is where the cattle made their break for it."

Several yards ahead, the barbed wire lay on the ground in long loose coils. Several of the metal fence posts had been knocked over and the wire had either been cut or had snapped.

"We'll need to clear this out a little more to get the cows through easily," Trace said.

"They found their way through the first time on their own," Matt pointed out.

"Yeah, but they had all day to pick their way through. I don't plan on taking all day getting them back. They're motivated easily by feed. I don't think we'll have a problem getting them back on this side." Trace dismounted and moved a strand of barbed wire to the side. Matt got down, stretched his legs and back, and started in on another strand, looping it back out of the way.

"You know," Trace said as he stood in the small gap they'd created, "we might want to find the cattle and get them started in this direction. While they're working their way back, we can get here ahead of them and clear their path."

"I'm game," Matt said.

The two men remounted, crossed onto the Rocking J Ranch and climbed to the top of a ridge.

From his vantage point, Trace could see down into a valley. "There," he said and pointed.

Several dozen cows grazed in the north corner of the valley.

"How are we going to get them from down there to

up here?" Matt asked. "Not to mention coaxing them through the fence."

Trace grinned. "They're used to being fed some grain through the winter. Granted, it's not winter, and they are feasting on green grass, but old habits die hard. All I should have to do is shake this bag of feed and they'll come running." He nudged his horse forward. "We have to get a little closer so they can see and hear us."

When they were within range, Trace whistled sharply and yelled, "Here, cow!"

Matt chuckled. "Really? They come to that?"

Several of the animals lifted their heads and stared in Trace's direction.

Trace untied the bag of feed from behind his saddle and held it up. "Here, cow!" And he shook the bag.

One cow let out a long mooing sound.

Another one answered. Neither moved.

Trace shook the feed bag again. "Here, cow!"

A number of steers looked up and took several steps in Trace's direction.

Again, Trace shook the feed bag. "Come on, don't make me come after you," he muttered.

Once two or three of the animals started in their direction, the others fell in line.

"Well, I'll be damned," Matt said.

"They're motivated by easy and tasty food." Trace ripped open the bag and poured a little on the ground.

Several of the cows mooed loudly and picked up the pace.

"Let's go," Trace said.

"Won't they stop when they find the grain on the ground?" Matt asked.

"I'll leave a trail of bread crumbs for them to follow," Trace said. "Or in this case, feed crumbs." He dribbled a little feed in a line heading up to the top of the ridge. "We need to get ahead of them and move more of the fence debris."

"On it." Matt passed Trace and topped the ridge.

With the cattle on the move, Trace and Matt hurried back to the gap in the fence, dismounted and went to work. The sound of cattle bellowing urged them to go faster.

Trace moved one of the posts back and forth, working the soil around it loose. When he pulled it out of the ground, something shiny glinted in the dirt. He bent to retrieve what appeared to be a silver coin. When he turned it over and saw the image of Susan B. Anthony on the front, his hand and heart froze.

Matt took the post from where Trace had left it and tossed it to the side. "Find something interesting?" He came to stand beside Trace and looked down at the coin. "I have a coin like that. Your—our father gave it to me." He reached into his pocket and pulled out one that looked just like the one in Trace's hand.

Trace reached into his own jeans pocket and pulled out another. "Dad gave me this one when I left to join the army. He said his always gave him good luck." He pointed to the dent on the edge. "It fell out of his pocket one day when he was working on an engine. It lodged in the sprockets and shut down the motor, saving him from losing several fingers." He met Matt's gaze.

"It was his, wasn't it?" Matt said softly.

Trace's eyes stung and his gut knotted. "Yeah. He never went anywhere without it." He glanced around. "This must have been where he was shot. He might have been working this fence when it happened." Trace looked around. "You take the Rocking J side. I'll take the Whiskey Gulch side. Look for a bullet casing."

"We don't know how far away the shooter was," Matt said. "He could have been yards away from here."

"The sheriff said the ME reported the shots were fired in an upward angle. Like someone pointing at him from the ground at close range. My father was in his saddle when he was hit."

For the next few minutes, they searched the area, kicking aside leaves, tufts of grass and barbed wire. They worked their way outward in a twenty-foot radius.

Matt finally straightened. "It's going to be impossible to find one casing—"

At that moment, Trace spied a shiny brass shell. "Found one! And here are two more."

Trace had bent over and was reaching for the first one when Matt called out, "Don't touch it." Matt hurried over to him, pulled a bandanna from his back pocket and bent to collect them, careful to lift the casings with the fabric of the handkerchief. "Sometimes they can collect fingerprints off the spent casings." Matt wrapped the casings in the cloth and handed them to Trace. "Let's get back to the house and call the sheriff."

As Trace mounted his horse, the cattle emerged from the tree line, headed their way, mooing as they came. Soon, Trace, Matt and the horses were surrounded by cows moving through the gap in the fence.

A loud crack sounded above the sound of the bellowing cows and Trace felt something sting the side of his arm.

"Get down!" Matt shouted.

Trace slipped out of his saddle and dropped to the ground among the herd.

Matt did the same, moving with the animals through the fence to the other side.

Another crack sounded and one of the steers let out a frightened bellow and started running.

Sensing the fear, the rest of the herd stampeded through the gap in the fence.

Matt and Trace dived to the side, away from the column of animals pushing through.

Trace pulled his weapon out of his shoulder holster and waited for the herd to move past so he could see to take aim. The shooter had the advantage. He'd seen them and knew generally where they were.

"We need to move toward the tree line before all the cattle get by," Trace yelled to Matt.

Trace crab-crawled backward, hugging the dirt, moving toward the trees. He prayed he and Matt would get there before their cover dispersed. Otherwise, they'd be easy targets for whoever wanted them dead.

"HURRY!" ROSALYNN URGED.

"Going as fast as I can," Lily said.

Irish winced at every rut they hit, since the SUV was going faster than the vehicle was designed to go over open fields with hidden potholes and dangerous rocks.

"Right," Rosalynn said from the back seat. "Go right. They were tracking along the fence bordering the Rocking J. That's to the north."

Lily jerked the steering wheel to the right and floored the accelerator. When they came to a fence, she turned left and drove through a narrow column between the fence and a stand of trees.

Irish tried to lean forward in his seat, but the seat belt was locked in place, keeping him firmly trapped in his seat.

In the distance Lily could see cattle stampeding through a break in the fence. "There!" she shouted. "Where the cows are running through the fence. Trace and Matt must be somewhere nearby." She strained to see the two men. As they drew nearer, she saw a horse running with the cattle. It had a saddle, but no rider.

"There's Lady," Rosalynn said. "Matt was riding her. Where's Matt?"

Lily saw Trace's black gelding race by, heading for the barn. "Where's Trace?" she asked as she stopped short of the herd of cattle.

Lily grabbed the gun from the glove box and shoved open her door.

Rosalynn leaned over the back of the seat and grabbed her arm. "Lily, you can't go out there. You'll be trampled."

Lily shook the hand from her arm. "If Trace and Matt have fallen off their horses, they'll be trampled. I can't let that happen." She slid out of the driver's seat and ran toward the fence. If Trace and Matt had fallen off their horses, it would have been because they'd been shot. They might not be able to move away from the cattle leaping through the gap in the fence.

Her breath caught on a sob as she raced toward the stampeding animals.

Irish called out behind her, "Lily! Wait! That's suicide!"

Suicide was a hell of a lot better option than to live after finding Trace dead. Now that he was back in her life, Lily didn't want to live without him—couldn't live without him. It would be more painful than being trampled to death by a herd of cattle.

The sound of an engine revving nearby made her turn her head long enough to see a four-wheeler dodging in and out of the stand of trees, heading in her direction.

Lily didn't have time to get out of the way.

The man on the ATV raced toward her, slowing long enough to reach out and grab her arm. He yanked her over the seat in front of him and gunned the accelerator, sending the vehicle leaping forward.

Lily landed hard on her belly across the man's knees, the breath knocked out of her lungs. When she could move again, she struggled to push out of his grip.

The ATV rocked back and forth as the driver struggled to hold on to her and steer at the same time. When he couldn't do both, he released the accelerator, threw her to the ground and dived on top of her. His helmet rolled off, exposing a shock of gray hair.

"I knew it," she cried.

"So now you're finally getting it," he growled as he twisted his hand in her hair. Then he jammed a handgun against her temple and backed up to the fence. "Just in time to be my ticket out of here."

The herd had crossed through the fence and continued toward the barn, leaving the clearing with the damaged fence in relative silence.

Lily scanned the ground, searching for Trace. She breathed a sigh when she didn't see a body trampled in the earth. "Why did you do it?" Lily leaned back, trying to ease the pain of having her hair pulled so hard it made her scalp hurt. "Why did you kill James?"

"Why should he have had it all? Land, money, a loving wife. He didn't deserve it. He didn't deserve her."

"And you did?"

"I worked hard, and for what?" His hand tightened in her hair.

Lily stood on her tiptoes to ease the pain.

"He fired me." Roy pushed the barrel of the pistol into her temple. "All because I was nice to his wife."

"The same way you were nice to Mrs. Talbot?" Lily asked.

"What do you know? She was going to marry me, and we would have run the ranch together." Roy dragged Lily several yards along the fence line, toward the gap. "Her son talked her out of it. Moved her to Florida and sold the ranch I was supposed to own."

"It wasn't yours," Lily said, trying to make conversation to distract him. To keep him from pulling the trigger.

"Whiskey Gulch should have been mine. I would have gotten away with it if the Travis brat hadn't come home. It would have been mine."

"And finding out the ranch wasn't going to Rosalynn put a kink in your plan?" Lily said.

"Who knew old man Travis had two kids? One was bad enough. At least he didn't want to run the ranch." Roy twisted his hand in her hair. "It doesn't matter. Once they're both out of the way, the ranch will revert to the rightful owner."

"To Rosalynn," Lily said. "And you think she will marry you?"

"Yes."

"After you kill her beloved son?" Lily forced a snort. "Face it, Roy. It's over."

"It's over when I say it's over." He pulled the gun away from her head, fired it into the air and pointed it again at her temple. "If you don't want the girl to die, you'll do as I say," Roy called out.

"What are you doing?" Lily searched the underbrush. Where were Trace and Matt?

"Gibson!" a voice called out from the direction Lily had come. Irish held up his hand. "Let her go. She's done nothing to hurt you."

"No, but she's going to get me out of here," he answered. "If her boyfriend isn't too much of a coward."

"Let her go, Roy." Trace stepped out from behind a tree three yards away from where Roy stood with Lily. He pointed his handgun at Roy's head.

"You won't shoot me as long as I have her," Roy said.

"Are you sure about that?" Trace asked.

"I have my finger on the trigger," Roy said. "All I have to do is squeeze and she's dead."

"What do you want, Roy?" Trace asked, his weapon still pointed at the man's head.

Roy shifted Lily, using her as a human shield. "I want it all. The ranch, the money, Rosalynn. Everything James had."

"You'll never have any of that." Rosalynn's voice came from Lily's right. "Not the ranch, not the money and certainly not me."

"But you liked me."

"I like everyone," Rosalynn said. "I loved my husband, and I love my son." She shook her head. "I could never love you, Roy. Ever," she said, her tone hard, her face angry. "You killed my soul mate. The only man I could ever love. I hope you rot in hell."

"It's over, Gibson," Matt said. "Put the gun down."

"We notified the sheriff," Lily lied. "He's on his way as we speak."

"Then I'll just have to take you with me." Roy tightened his hold on Lily's hair.

Anger surged inside Lily. Her gaze met Trace's.

Trace frowned. "Lily?"

Tired of being a victim, Lily did what she'd been taught in a self-defense class. She went limp in Roy's arms and sank in front of him.

His hand still knotted in her hair, he had to move the gun pressed to her temple in order not to be dragged down with her.

Lily ducked her head, squeezed her eyes shut and prayed.

Shots rang out.

She couldn't tell if it was two or three. She waited for the pain. It didn't come.

Roy's grip on her hair loosened. He swayed and finally he fell, his body landing on top of Lily, crushing the air from her lungs.

Something warm and wet spread across her back. She struggled to move Roy off her, but his dead weight trapped her beneath him.

Then the weight was gone and Trace dropped to his knees beside her. "Lily, sweetheart, are you okay?" His hands roamed over her body. When his fingers swept over the damp spot on her back, he froze. "Dear sweet heaven, you're hurt."

Relieved she could breathe, she pushed to a sitting position.

"Don't move. We need to apply pressure to the wound." He tried to guide her back to a prone position.

Lily shook her head. "I'm okay," she assured him. "I'm not hurt."

"But the blood," Trace said. "There's so much."

"It's not mine." She managed to sit upright, despite Trace's attempts to keep her from doing so. "Really, I'm okay. None of the shots fired hit me." She glanced toward Roy. "Who got him?"

"I did," Trace, Irish and Matt answered as one.

Rosalynn knelt between Lily and Roy. "Are you all right?" she asked Lily.

Lily nodded. "I can't say the same for Roy."

The older woman stared down at the foreman, her eyes sad. "What gave him the idea he could kill my husband and then marry me?"

Matt joined her and slipped an arm around her shoulders. "He was a sick man."

Lily leaned into Trace. "It's over," she whispered.

He nodded and touched his lips to the top of her head. "Yes, it is."

"DOES THIS MEAN you're heading back to active duty?" Lily held her breath, praying he would say no.

"Only for a little while. I need to put in for separation. I was due to reenlist next month." He pushed to his feet and held out his hand to Lily.

She took it and let him pull her up and into his arms. "And now? Do you want to stay in the military for another nine years to get your twenty?"

Trace glanced around at the people surrounding them. "I think not. I'm needed here."

Lily blinked, shocked by his answer, but afraid it was all a joke, or that she was asleep and when she opened her eyes, she'd wake to an alternate outcome.

He held her at arm's length. "I want to stay," he said. "But only if you stay with me."

Lily's eyes widened and a smile tugged at her lips. "Stay with you?" Her grin broadened. "Wild horses couldn't drag me away."

He pulled her close and crushed her lips with his. "I was so afraid I'd miss," Trace said. "I couldn't live without you. Not again."

"*You* were afraid *you'd* miss." Matt laughed, the sound harsh and without humor.

"I'm glad none of us missed," Irish said, clutching a hand to his midsection. "And, please, don't drive back as fast as we drove here. I don't think my insides can take it."

Rosalynn patted Irish's back. "Thank you. I don't know what we would have done without you."

"I caught most of what Roy said to you." Trace shook his head and glanced at his mother. "I can't believe he thought you'd marry him after losing Dad."

"The man was clearly insane." Rosalynn stared at Roy's body. "If I'd had a gun on me, mine would have been the fourth bullet. For my husband and…" She reached for Lily's hand. "For the woman who has become a daughter to me. I love you, Lily."

Lily smiled at Rosalynn through blurred eyes. "I love you, too."

"I'll stay with the body," Matt said, "while the rest of you head back to the ranch house and wait for the sheriff."

Trace shook his head. "I'll take the four-wheeler back to the barn for the supplies and tools we'll need. Despite the circumstances, we need to get the fence patched."

Lily hugged him around the waist. "I know how to work a come-along," Lily offered. "I'll go with you."

Irish offered his arm to Rosalynn. "That leaves the two of us for heading back to the house."

"We'll call the sheriff and start supper," Rosalynn said. "When the sheriff arrives, I'll send Irish out with him to find you."

"Sounds like a good plan." Trace pressed a kiss to his mother's cheek. "Are you all right?"

She nodded. "I will be." Her gaze dropped to Roy's inert form. "I just wish I'd seen the signs."

"He was good at hiding his dark thoughts," Lily said. "I didn't see it, either."

"Come on," Trace said. "The sooner the sheriff comes to collect Roy and we get that fence done, the sooner we get to go back to the house." He hopped onto the four-wheeler Roy had ridden and scooted forward, giving Lily room to ride behind him.

Lily wrapped her arms around Trace's waist and pressed her cheek against his back. She hadn't been this happy in…well, in eleven years. Now that she and Trace were back together, she didn't care where they ended up, as long as they had each other.

Epilogue

"I've been thinking," Trace said as he sat on the porch swing, looking out over the barn and the pastures beyond.

"That's a dangerous pastime for a former Delta Force soldier." Matt leaned against a porch post, chewing on a strand of hay.

"No kidding," Irish said. "Every time Trace started thinking, we ended up knee-deep in enemy territory."

"Seriously, I think Matt was right. Adjusting to civilian life might be harder than we think," Trace said.

Lily frowned beside Trace. "Does that mean you're going to sell and go back on active duty?"

Trace squeezed her hand. "No. But I think we can manage the ranch, keep our combat skills current and help others."

"How do you figure we can do all that?" Irish asked.

"I'd like to form a security service to help people who can't get the justice they deserve for whatever reason."

Matt crossed his arms over his chest. "Are you talking about a vigilante group?" He shook his head. "If you are, count me out."

"No. I'm talking about people the law or the government aren't helping because they don't have the resources or time. Folks who need a private investigator, bodyguard or security detail."

"And you want the three of us to manage that while managing a ranch?" Irish raised his eyebrows. "Sounds like a lot."

Trace grinned. "No. I think this concept can be a lot bigger than the three of us. I want to bring on others like us, men and women who have special fighting skills. It will help others while helping our military personnel who have separated from service for one reason or another."

Irish leaned forward. "People like me who are good with a gun and not much else?"

Trace laughed. "Mom says you're a budding chef."

"I can cook a pot of chili," Irish said. "I'm not a chef. But I could really get into being a private investigator or bodyguard."

"Same here," Matt said. "The auto repair business doesn't keep me nearly busy enough to maintain my sanity."

Trace clapped his hands together. "Then we're all in?"

Irish and Matt nodded.

"Now all we need is a name for this organization."

"How about Outriders?" Irish said.

Trace shook his head. "We're not all cowboys or mounted heroes, but I like the ring to it."

Rosalynn stepped out on the porch, carrying a tray full of glasses and a pitcher of iced tea. "I like it." She set the tray on the table, poured tea into a glass and handed it to Trace.

He stared at his mother as he took the cup from her hand.

"What?" she said.

"I like it," Trace said. "It doesn't matter that you're not all cowboys. You're ex-soldiers who want to help and protect those in need."

Lily smiled beside him. "I think it's perfect. You might not all be cowboys, but if you hire all former military, they're all heroes. For serving this country."

Trace raised his eyebrows and looked around at Matt and Irish. "Agreed on the name?"

They nodded.

"Done," Trace said. "Now all we need is to hire more resources and get started with our first case."

Matt took the glass Rosalynn handed him. "I think I have the first case, if you want to test our facilities and communication skills."

"What is it?" Trace asked.

Matt stared across at him, their gazes locking. "I want to investigate the murder of Heather Hennessey."

"A relative?" Trace asked.

"My mother," Matt said.

For a long moment, the people sitting or standing on the front porch paused in silence.

Trace nodded. "So be it. We'll start by finding Heather Hennessey's murderer." He stood and held out his hand to Matt. "Welcome to the Outriders."

Matt pushed away from the post and took Trace's hand in a firm grip. "I don't know about cowboys on horseback, but as long as I can ride my motorcycle, I'm in."

"You got it." Trace pulled him close for a quick hug. "I'm still getting used to the fact I have a brother."

"Half," Matt corrected and hugged him back.

Trace turned to Irish. "And my other brother in arms…" He held out a hand.

Irish took it and pulled him straight into a bone-crushing hug. "I've got your back."

With a grin, Trace turned to Lily and held out a hand.

Lily chuckled. "Are you inviting me into this little bromance you're having?"

"Looks like it. Hell, with you by my side, we'll be unstoppable." He drew her to her feet and slipped an arm around her waist.

Lily tipped her head back and raised her eyebrows. "Will you be accepting applications from cowgirls?"

"You know it," Trace answered. "I *know* I like *you*."

"About time you realized it," she murmured.

Trace brushed a strand of her hair back from her forehead. "I've always known it."

"You two should get a room," Irish said.

"Trust Irish to say what's on my mind." Trace bent and pressed a kiss to Lily's lips. "Now, if the rest of you will excuse us…we have eleven years of catching up to do."

His mother grinned as they passed her, headed for the door. "That's right. I want grandchildren before I'm too old to appreciate them."

Trace threw a thumbs-up over his shoulder as he stepped across the threshold. "Working on it."

* * * * *

WE HOPE YOU ENJOYED
THIS BOOK FROM

HARLEQUIN

INTRIGUE

Seek thrills. Solve crimes. Justice served.

Dive into action-packed stories that will keep you
on the edge of your seat. Solve the crime
and deliver justice at all costs.

6 NEW BOOKS AVAILABLE EVERY MONTH!

Prologue

The tears leaked out of Kay Duvall's eyes, even as she tried to
focus on what she had to do. *Had* to do to bring Ben home safe.

She fumbled with her ID and punched in the code that
would open the side door, usually only used for a guard taking a
smoke break. It would be easy for the men behind her to escape
from this side of the prison.

It went against everything she was supposed to do.
Everything she considered right and good.

A quiet sob escaped her lips. They had her son. How could
she not help them escape? Nothing mattered beyond her son's
life.

"Would you stop already?" one of the prisoners muttered.
He'd made her give him her gun, which he now jabbed into her
back. "Crying isn't going to change anything. So just shut up."

She didn't care so much about her own life or if she'd be
fired. She didn't care what happened to her as long as they let
her son go. So she swallowed down the sobs and blinked out as
many tears as she could, hoping to stem the tide of them.

She got the door open and slid out first—because the man holding the gun pushed it into her back until she moved forward.

They came through the door behind her, dressed in the clothes she'd stolen from the locker room and Lost and Found. Anything warm she could get her hands on to help them escape into the frigid February night.

Help them escape. Help three dangerous men escape prison. When she was supposed to keep them inside.

It didn't matter anymore. She just wanted them gone. If they were gone, they'd let her baby go. They had to let her baby go.

Kay forced her legs to move, one foot in front of the other, toward the gate she could unlock without setting off any alarms. She unlocked it, steadier this time if only because she kept thinking that once they were gone, she could get in contact with Ben.

She flung open the gate and gestured them out into the parking lot. "Stay out of the safety lights and no one should bug you."

"You better hope not," one of the men growled.

"The minute you sound that alarm, your kid is dead. You got it?" This one was the ringleader. The one who'd been in for murder. Who else would he kill out there in the world?

Guilt pooled in Kay's belly, but she had to ignore it. She had to live with it. Whatever guilt she felt would be survivable. Living without her son wouldn't be. Besides, she had to believe they'd be caught. They'd do something else terrible and be caught.

As long as her son was alive, she didn't care.

Don't miss
Hunting a Killer *by Nicole Helm,*
available February 2021 wherever
Harlequin Intrigue books and ebooks are sold.

Harlequin.com

HIEXP0121

Get 4 FREE REWARDS!

We'll send you 2 FREE Books plus 2 FREE Mystery Gifts.

Harlequin Intrigue books are action-packed stories that will keep you on the edge of your seat. Solve the crime and deliver justice at all costs.

FREE
Value Over
$20

Love Harlequin romance?

DISCOVER.

Be the first to find out about promotions, news and exclusive content!

 Facebook.com/HarlequinBooks

Twitter.com/HarlequinBooks

Instagram.com/HarlequinBooks

Pinterest.com/HarlequinBooks

ReaderService.com

EXPLORE.

Sign up for the Harlequin e-newsletter and download a free book from any series at **TryHarlequin.com**

CONNECT.

Join our Harlequin community to share your thoughts and connect with other romance readers! **Facebook.com/groups/HarlequinConnection**

HSOCIAL2020

HARLEQUIN

Heartfelt or suspenseful, inspiring or passionate, Harlequin has your happily-ever-after.

With new books published every month, you are sure to find the satisfying escape you know you deserve.

HNEWS2020